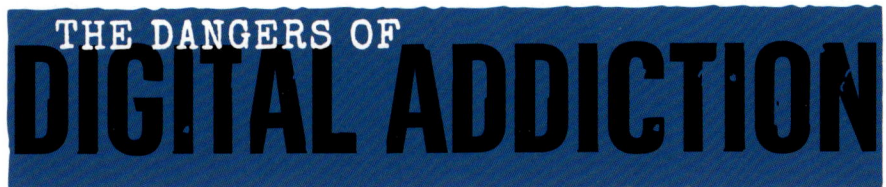

THE DANGERS OF DIGITAL ADDICTION

By Amanda Vink

Published in 2020 by
Lucent Press, an Imprint of Greenhaven Publishing, LLC
353 3rd Avenue
Suite 255
New York, NY 10010

Copyright © 2020 Lucent Press, an Imprint of Greenhaven Publishing, LLC.

All rights reserved. No part of this book may be reproduced in any form without permission in writing from the publisher, except by a reviewer.

Designer: Deanna Paternostro
Editor: Jennifer Lombardo

Library of Congress Cataloging-in-Publication Data

Names: Vink, Amanda, author.
Title: The dangers of digital addiction / Amanda Vink.
Description: New York : Lucent Press, [2020] | Series: Hot topics | Includes bibliographical references and index.
Identifiers: LCCN 2019004548 (print) | LCCN 2019010575 (ebook) | ISBN 9781534567665 (eBook) | ISBN 9781534567658 (paperback) | ISBN 9781534567016 (library bound book)
Subjects: LCSH: Internet addiction–Juvenile literature. | Social media addiction–Juvenile literature.
Classification: LCC RC569.5.I54 (ebook) | LCC RC569.5.I54 V56 2020 (print) | DDC 616.85/84–dc23
LC record available at https://lccn.loc.gov/2019004548

Printed in the United States of America

CPSIA compliance information: Batch #BS19KL: For further information contact Greenhaven Publishing LLC, New York, New York at 1-844-317-7404.

Please visit our website, www.greenhavenpublishing.com. For a free color catalog of all our high-quality books, call toll free 1-844-317-7404 or fax 1-844-317-7405.

CONTENTS

FOREWORD	4
INTRODUCTION Changing Times	6
CHAPTER 1 Technology in the Modern Age	11
CHAPTER 2 What Is an Addiction?	25
CHAPTER 3 Technology Taking Over	40
CHAPTER 4 Signs of an Addiction	64
CHAPTER 5 Living in a Digital World	74
NOTES	89
DISCUSSION QUESTIONS	94
ORGANIZATIONS TO CONTACT	96
FOR MORE INFORMATION	98
INDEX	100
PICTURE CREDITS	103
ABOUT THE AUTHOR	104

Adolescence is a time when many people begin to take notice of the world around them. News channels, blogs, and talk radio shows are constantly promoting one view or another; very few are unbiased. Young people also hear conflicting information from parents, friends, teachers, and acquaintances. Often, they will hear only one side of an issue or be given flawed information. People who are trying to support a particular viewpoint may cite inaccurate facts and statistics on their blogs, and news programs present many conflicting views of important issues in our society. In a world where it seems everyone has a platform to share their thoughts, it can be difficult to find unbiased, accurate information about important issues.

It is not only facts that are important. In blog posts, in comments on online videos, and on talk shows, people will share opinions that are not necessarily true or false, but can still have a strong impact. For example, many young people struggle with their body image. Seeing or hearing negative comments about particular body types online can have a huge effect on the way someone views himself or herself and may lead to depression and anxiety. Although it is important not to keep information hidden from young people under the guise of protecting them, it is equally important to offer encouragement on issues that affect their mental health.

The titles in the Hot Topics series provide readers with different viewpoints on important issues in today's society. Many of these issues, such as gang violence and gun control laws, are of immediate concern to young people. This series aims to give readers factual context on these crucial topics in a way that lets them form their own opinions. The facts presented throughout also serve to empower readers to help themselves or support people they know who are struggling with many of the challenges adolescents face today. Although negative viewpoints are not ignored or downplayed, this series allows young people to see that the challenges they face are not insurmountable. As increasing numbers of young adults join political debates, especially regarding gun violence, learning the facts as well as the views of others will help them decide where they stand—and understand what they are fighting for.

Quotes encompassing all viewpoints are presented and cited so readers can trace them back to their original source, verifying for themselves whether the information comes from a reputable place. Additional books and websites are listed, giving readers a starting point from which to continue their own research. Chapter questions encourage discussion, allowing young people to hear and understand their classmates' points of view as they further solidify their own. Full-color photographs and enlightening charts provide a deeper understanding of the topics at hand. All of these features augment the informative text, helping young people understand the world they live in and formulate their own opinions concerning the best way they can improve it.

INTRODUCTION

Changing Times

New technologies have always reshaped the world. In the last few decades of the 20th century, digital technologies became more integrated into everyday life and changed the world once again. Today, people carry their smartphones with them everywhere, and through these mobile devices, they can stay connected almost all the time. Although many young people find it difficult to remember a time when they did not have Google at their fingertips or the ability to send and receive instantaneous texts, this is a relatively new development. In 1962, the first active communications satellite was launched from Cape Canaveral in Florida. The satellite, called Telstar, was able to send and receive signals by antenna. This breakthrough helped launch a communications revolution, giving people the ability to send information faster and farther than ever before. This technology has been improved and expanded over the years, and today, lightning-fast communication has become commonplace—and it has changed the ways people spend their daily lives.

Experts debate the consequences the changing digital landscape has had and will continue to have on individuals. Some people are excited for digital technology's role in improving the human condition. Others worry that digital technology is contributing to a society where people lose what makes them human in the first place. These people fear humans will no longer talk to one another and that the technology that was supposed to connect everyone has actually disconnected humans from the natural world. Even worse, some people believe digital technologies are bad for human health and are easy to become addicted to.

People argue whether technology is good or bad. However, technology itself is not intrinsically, or naturally, good or bad. Instead, what makes technology good or bad for people is the intent behind a device, how it is designed to be used, and how it is actually used. "At their best," wrote Clive Thompson in his book *Smarter Than You Think: How Technology Is Changing Our Minds for the Better*, "today's digital tools help us see more, retain more, communicate more. At their worst, they leave us prey to the manipulation of the toolmakers."[1] When toolmakers such as application, or app, designers do not think about the way their designs interact with users—or worse, when toolmakers actively try to manipulate users—that is when technology can become dangerous.

Skeptics of technology have been raging against new devices or practices for as long as humans have created new inventions. For example, it is believed the scholar Socrates was skeptical of writing because he believed it would encourage humans not to exercise memory and because written words are not as easily adaptable to different groups of people as spoken ones. These arguments were, ironically, written down by his student Plato. The printing press, too, was praised by some and scorned by others. Many people were thrilled because books, which had once been so scarce and expensive that only the very wealthy could own them, suddenly became widely available. However, some people feared that so many books would now be printed that society would be drowning in a giant pile of books. Similarly, some modern people wonder how all the information coming and going on screens will be sifted through in the future.

John H. Lienhard, a mechanical engineer at the University of Houston, gave a lecture in which he made the point that in many ways, whether people think new technologies are positive or negative does not matter much. He said, "What did they say in 1498? In the end it doesn't matter, because it was ... useless commentary. For everyone looking at the new books in 1498, the future was as hopelessly unpredictable as it is now. We cannot have a clue as to what any technological future will be until we learn it from a new generation of users."[2] In other words, to know how new technologies will affect the population, it is necessary to wait and see.

Of course, that does not mean people should not be critical of objects that are used every day. Some scholars believe there is a difference between the latest inventions and the ones of the past; they fear that there is a very real chance that digital technology has or will become more enticing than life away from that technology. Susan Greenfield, author of *Mind Change: How Digital Technologies Are Leaving Their Marks on Our Brains*, wrote that in contrast to previous inventions, digital technology is not a means to an end: "A car gets you from place to place; a fridge keeps your food fresh; a book can help you learn about the real world and the people in it. But digital technology has the potential to become the end rather than the means, a lifestyle all on its own."[3]

Although many people have ideas about how digital technologies will change the world and the people in it, it is still too early to tell whose predictions will come true. More research, especially in neuroscience and how the brain functions, will hopefully reveal more and allow scientists and technology developers to map out the best way to use technology so it is as helpful as possible for its users. In the meantime, it is important for people to recognize that there can be a negative effect of too much technology. When the use of technology starts to take over a person's life, this can be considered an addiction.

How Tech Giants Use Technology

Technology is only as good as the people who make it and the people who control it. Some side effects are already being seen, both positive and negative. Many people are increasingly reliant on technology, causing them to spend large chunks of time on cell phones, laptops, and tablets. It is becoming clear that understanding how to use technology responsibly is the key.

It is interesting to note that many of the world's leading tech innovators have not allowed their children unlimited access to digital technologies. They set limits because they know being online can easily get out of hand. For example, Steve Jobs, the cofounder of Apple, admitted to the *New York Times* in 2010 that he did not allow his children to use the iPad. "We limit how much technology our kids use at home,"[4] he explained.

Other parents living and working in Silicon Valley—the nickname given to part of the Bay Area of San Francisco, California, where most technology companies are located—are doing the same thing. "The approach stems from parents seeing firsthand, either through their job, or simply by living in the Bay Area ... how much time and effort goes into making digital technology irresistible,"[5] wrote Chris Weller in *Business Insider*. Digital technology is addictive by design, but does that mean people are actually addicted?

Silicon Valley (shown here) is the heart of the tech industry in the United States. It is located in the southern San Francisco Bay Area in Northern California.

According to a study from the University of Hong Kong, an estimated 6 percent of the world's population—roughly

420 million people—is addicted to the internet. That does not take into account the many people who are not addicted but spend too much time online. Other people argue that a person cannot be addicted to something that is not a substance that causes a synthetic chemical change within the body. Others who do not believe in digital addiction argue that something that affects such a large part of the population cannot be an addiction. In the United States, digital addiction is not yet listed as a medical disorder, but a few other countries, such as China, have classified it this way.

With so many conflicting viewpoints and opinions, it can be difficult to judge how digital technologies actually affect society. This difficulty is increased by the fact that, because the technologies of today are still so new, there are no studies that can accurately predict how human development is affected when young children are constantly exposed to technology. Not enough time has passed for long-term studies to be completed, so experts may not have firm answers for another few decades—if they ever get them at all. One thing is certain: Digital technologies are not going away. There is no easy way to get rid of them completely, and even if there was, most people would not be likely to allow it to happen. Instead, people must learn to adapt to new technologies and use them in as healthy a way as possible. The coming years will likely be full of many conversations about digital technology and digital addiction. Some of these conversations may even impact the technology industry as a whole, and they will certainly shape the way people use digital technologies.

Technology in the Modern Age

In 2017, more than a quarter of a billion new users came online for the first time. In 2018, more than 4 billion people around the world—half the world's total population—had access to the internet. The number of people using digital technologies will continue to grow as access to devices and the internet also continues to grow. While some countries lack the infrastructure to quickly make the internet available to all citizens, there are efforts to lay cable and launch new satellites. Programs such as CSquared are building a web presence in places such as Uganda and Ghana by installing fiber optic cables.

In the United States, the average person spends 6 hours and 30 minutes on the internet per day. Thailand has the highest average usage, clocking in at 9 hours and 38 minutes, while Morocco has the lowest among the countries studied at 2 hours and 53 minutes. In the United States, 98 percent of young adults ages 18 to 29 use the internet, and 97 percent of adults ages 30 to 49 use the internet. On the extreme ends of the spectrum, 11 percent of Americans do not use the internet at all, while 26 percent of American adults reported they are almost constantly online, both at home and at work.

Many jobs now rely on digital technologies, which have had the benefit of making a lot of jobs faster. Transactions can be made instantly, and people can email from anywhere. For example, it used to be that a newspaper would come every morning or weekend. People could listen to the radio for news in between, but receiving information was much slower. Now, information is recorded as things happen. Often, reporters do not know about something that is happening until a witness streams video footage or writes about it on social media. Many government processes are now live-streamed: In

Vocational Training for Tech Jobs

According to the U.S. Bureau of Labor Statistics, more than 50 percent of jobs today require some use of technology. In the 2020s, that number is predicted to increase to 77 percent. To ensure that young adults are able to get jobs after they finish school, educational opportunities will likely need to shift and become more available to a wider range of people. While some jobs involve mostly unskilled labor that people can pick up quickly as they practice it, working with computers and other types of technology generally requires specialized training. Not everyone can afford to go to college, but as this area of the job market opens up and more employees are needed to fill those positions, vocational training has become more available.

Vocational training is a phrase that describes education that teaches a specific skill set needed to perform a certain job. In contrast, college students take general education courses and electives, or classes that sound interesting to them but are not required, as well as classes that are specific to their major. Vocational training is generally more affordable than a college degree, making it more accessible to people from a variety of backgrounds. For technology jobs, vocational training focuses on "solid fundamental skills—literacy, numeracy, digital literacy—and relevant technology skills, such as the ability to troubleshoot a computer network or to write code."[1] Most elementary schools are also now starting to introduce coding classes alongside their general computer education courses, helping kids build a foundation for tech jobs at a very young age.

1. Fiona Macaulay, "Technology Skills Training Critical to Employ Low-Income Youth," Devex, September 22, 2014. www.devex.com/news/technology-skills-training-critical-to-employ-low-income-youth-84377.

2018, for example, people across the United States watched Dr. Christine Blasey Ford testify against U.S. Supreme Court then-nominee Brett Kavanaugh before the Senate Judiciary Committee in regard to her allegations that he had sexually assaulted her several years prior. While it was happening, social media feeds lit up with the opinions of thousands.

Computers, mobile devices, and the internet have allowed humans to develop intelligent process automation, which means artificial intelligence (AI) has been inserted into many systems people use every day. The goal is to have computers take over the mindless tasks that keep many workers bogged down. Automation frees up a worker's time, and it also makes human errors—for example, hitting the wrong button on a keyboard—less likely to happen. In addition to saving time, intelligent process automation can be monitored and changes that make life easier for workers can be made in real time.

The Information Age

In 2018, neurosurgeon Dr. Kurtis Auguste used virtual reality to create a 3-D model of one of his patient's brains. Using this model, Auguste was better able to plan and actually walk through the brain surgery prior to making any incisions, or cuts. His patient, a young man named Mathias, had a blood clot in his brain that had paralyzed him and caused him to lose the ability to speak. After surgery, he recovered. Auguste gave some credit to the technology, saying, "It allows us vantage points that are simply impossible to achieve by any other means. Equipped with these tools, neurosurgical planning has never been safer or more comprehensive. This technology made all the difference for this patient's case and made an invaluable contribution to the success of his surgery."[6]

In addition to this type of practical and life-saving application, technology has changed people's everyday lives. One of the most noticeable is that, through technology, humans can be more connected than ever. FaceTime, Skype, and other video apps allow geographically scattered family members and friends to connect with and see one another. According to the Pew Research Center, 59 percent of teens

Users of virtual reality see a three-dimensional world through headsets similar to the one shown here.

video chat with their friends, and 79 percent of teens instant message with their friends. Computers allow people to work in many fields that do not have physical offices near them. In 2018, 5.2 percent of Americans worked from home, up from 3.3 percent in 2000.

The 21st century has been nicknamed the Information Age or the Digital Age because there has been a shift from traditional industry, or labor that creates actual products, to information technology. Even traditional businesses need to use digital technologies to stay relevant. For example, a plumber may need to create a website to continue getting customers, which means they may need to hire a website designer.

It is difficult to say exactly when the Information Age began; some people say it was in the 1960s when there began to be more white-collar workers, or office workers, than blue-collar workers, or people who perform manual labor. Others pinpoint the timeframe in the 1970s, when tech companies such as Apple were starting to grow, while others believe it started in the 1990s, when personal computers became more widely available. People started sending electronic mail, or email, and looking information up online. The wider availability of technology also broadened educational opportunities; for example, many people now earn college degrees online at home.

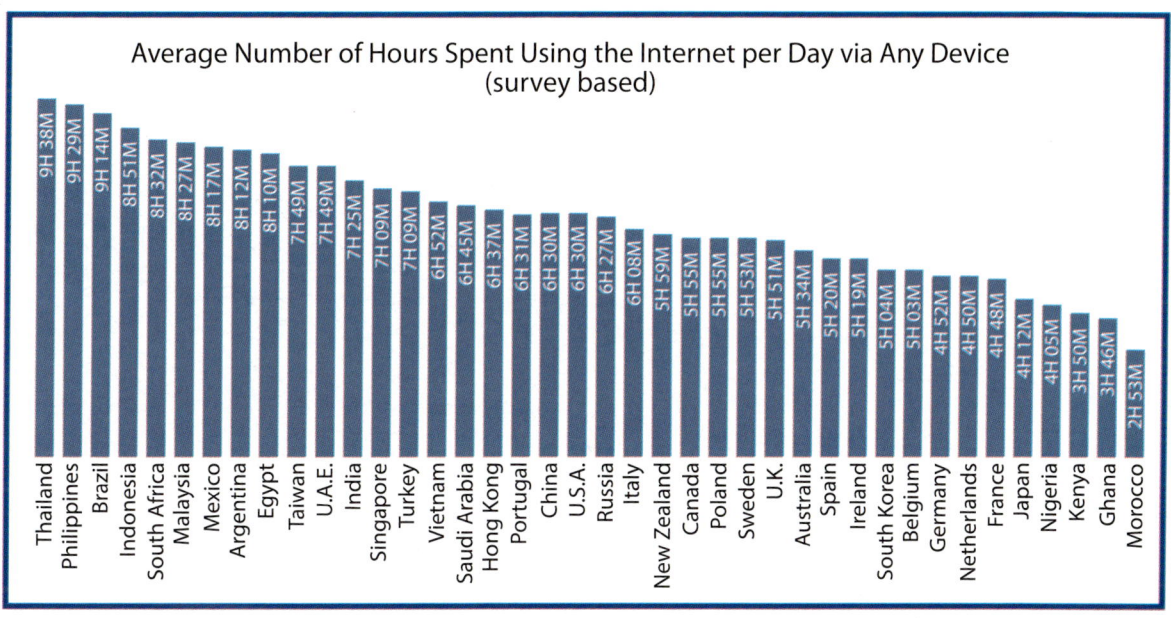

In January 2018, the Global Web Index surveyed internet users between the ages of 16 and 64. As their information shows, people in Thailand spent the most time online and people in Morocco spent the least amount of time. The United States fell roughly in the middle with an average of 6 hours (H) and 30 minutes (M) per day.

The Internet

The internet is the result of a collaboration among many scientists, programmers, and engineers. While many people had ideas about the development of a wireless communication system, the groundwork really began to be laid in the 1960s when J. C. R. Licklider, an American psychologist and computer scientist, popularized the idea of a network of computers.

The first working prototype of the internet was called the Advanced Research Projects Agency Network (ARPANET), which was originally funded by the U.S. Department of Defense. The system used packet switching, a method for transmitting electronic data, to allow multiple computers to communicate on one network. In the 1970s, scientists Robert Kahn and Vinton Cerf created Transmission Control Protocol/Internet Protocol (TCP/IP), which allowed data to be transferred between different networks.

The World Wide Web, the most common way data is accessed online, was created in 1989 by Tim Berners-Lee and became available to the general public in 1990. This is what helped make the internet so popular. A common misconception is that the World Wide Web and the internet are the same thing, but in reality, the internet is the connection between the computers and the World Wide Web is the way people access information that is stored on the internet. When people look something up on Google, check their social media, or watch videos on YouTube, they are using the internet to access the World Wide Web. However, the two words are still frequently used interchangeably.

At first, people connected to the internet through their phone lines. In this process, which was called dial-up, the analog signals were converted to digital by a modem and sent through the telephone wires. DSL, or Digital Subscriber Line, is an internet connection that uses two telephone connections, which allows subscribers to use the internet and the phone at the same time. Before DSL, a dial-up connection would tie up the phone line so no one could make or receive calls while someone else was using the internet. Cable internet operates through a cable modem and over cable television lines.

Within only a few years, however, people figured out ways to access the internet without any wires at all. Wireless

Technology in the Modern Age

Tim Berners-Lee is the inventor of the World Wide Web.

methods use satellites, radio waves, and cell towers to send signals to devices such as smartphones and computers. When new ways of providing the internet to people are discovered, it is called a "generation." For example, 5G represents the fifth generation of internet technology. Each generation is faster and more reliable than the ones that came before it.

The Rise of the Smartphone

Today, people can carry the internet with them at all times on their phone. However, this was not always the case. The plans for the first basic phone were created in 1849 by Italian inventor Antonio Meucci. However, it was Alexander Graham Bell who won the first U.S. patent in 1876. Between 1877 and 1878, the first telephone line was constructed and the first switchboard was created to transfer calls between phones. In 1880, the American Bell Telephone Company came into existence. Later, in 1885, it evolved into the American Telegraph and Telephone Company (AT&T).

THE INVENTION OF THE INTERNET

"The internet is the first thing that humanity has built that humanity doesn't understand, the largest experiment in anarchy that we have ever had."

–Eric Schmidt, former executive chairman of Google

Quoted in Jerome Taylor, "Google Chief: My Fears for Generation Facebook," *Independent*, August 18, 2010. www.independent.co.uk/life-style/gadgets-and-tech/news/google-chief-my-fears-for-generation-facebook-2055390.html.

AT&T had a huge monopoly on the telephone industry—one that lasted many years. For the most part, the telephone industry was private, except during World War I, when telephones were put under the direction of the U.S. Postal Service (USPS). In an effort to make phone service more efficient, USPS combined different networks and exempted AT&T from government antitrust laws. By the 1960s, there were more than 80 million phone hookups in the United States. An antitrust suit was filed in 1974, and since the war effort was long over, AT&T was forced to sell business interests in order to make the playing field more level. This made it easier for the first cellular networks to come online in 1993,

Fiber Optics

Fiber optic cables—the fastest way to provide internet access as of 2019—make up a huge part of communications technology. Verizon Fios and Google Fiber both use fiber optic technology, as do multiple other internet service providers (ISPs).

Fiber optics uses thin, flexible fibers to send light signals that also transmit data. This means fiber optics users are literally sending information at the speed of light. The technology was invented by Robert Maurer, Donald Keck, and Peter Schultz. All three were researchers at Corning, a company that specializes in technologies made from glass, ceramics, and other non-metal materials. Fiber optic cables can carry 65,000 times more information than copper wire, which is how internet data was transmitted when dial-up was in use.

Fiber optic cables (top) are made up of bundles of thin, light-carrying fibers (bottom).

Alexander Graham Bell was the first person to patent the telephone.

and two years later, there were 25 million cell phone users in the United States.

Cell phones today are a lot like small computers. They have central processing units and screens. In addition, many smartphones have internal memory to store data, sensors, and cameras. A cell phone call works by tapping into cell towers, which have been placed all around the world. New York City alone has so many cellular antennas that officials have actually lost track of the number.

Towers such as the ones shown here allow people to connect to digital technologies without the use of wires.

Too Much?

According to the Pew Research Center, a typical U.S. home of three people has 24 technological gadgets, including at least one cell phone. There are actually more cell phones in the United States than there are people because many adults have one for personal use and one for work. It is estimated that 67 percent of the world's population will have cell phones by 2019. Nearly all cell phones in industrialized countries allow users to connect to the internet, play games, and watch videos in addition to their original purpose of making communication easier through calls and texts. When people carry these devices everywhere, it generally becomes second nature to pull the phone out any time someone is bored or fidgety.

There has been growing concern over the amount of time people spend online. People do depend on technology for a lot of modern comforts, but when does a dependency become an addiction?

Without a doubt, there are a lot of positives to having technology incorporated into daily life. One of the biggest pluses is the way it can be used to help people remember things. Computers allow humans to store and retrieve all sorts of information quickly, and unlike paper and ink, a digital copy does not disintegrate and does not change. When someone recalls something, such as an event that happened or a quote they once read, the mind fills in any blanks, which sometimes alters a memory in a big way. Often, when two people are remembering a particular event, they each remember it differently. This is not because one person is lying—it is because the human brain has limitations. When someone calls up a memory, certain brain networks involved in this process can cause details to change. The next time the person calls up the same memory, instead of remembering what originally happened, they remember what the memory was like the last time they recalled it. Having technology available at all times allows people to record certain things so they can remember exactly what happened. It can also keep them from forgetting important dates and appointments. This way, brain space is freed up to store more important memories.

   Some people see this as a good thing, while others fear that overreliance on technology for this purpose has negative effects on a person's ability to remember things. The theory is that if people know they can simply look something up on their phone later, they will not bother to even try to remember what they have just learned, whether it is an important fact or someone's phone number. Some experts say this can affect

Some people fear that humans have become too dependent on digital technologies such as cell phones.

> ## POSITIVES AND NEGATIVES
>
> "There are innumerable advantages of technology in society, especially in the medical and science fields. It has arguably had an incredibly positive impact on the quality of life thus far. However, like anything in life, technology is only safe in moderation … Technology in excess can have an isolating and destructive effect on society."
>
> –Julia Martin, writer for the *Odyssey*

Julia Martin, "Technology: The Good, the Bad, and the Ugly," *Odyssey*, October 19, 2015. www.theodysseyonline.com/technology-the-good-the-bad-and-the-ugly.

a person's short-term memory, which can then cause problems with someone's long-term memory. While not having to remember unimportant details can be a benefit of technology, an inability to remember most things can have serious negative effects on a person's overall brain function and ability to make intelligent decisions. In recent years, there has been much debate about how much digital technology usage is too much, how exactly the brain is affected, and whether overreliance on technology can be considered an addiction.

What Is an Addiction?

Opinion articles, news stories, and other media that questions if people are addicted to their digital devices can be found everywhere. This question is not easily answered, and while some people note the uncertainty around this topic, others confidently proclaim that there is one true answer, even in the absence of hard data. One of the sources of confusion is the way people talk about technology: Often, people say they are addicted to their phones, sometimes truthfully and sometimes jokingly. It can be difficult to judge whether a dependence on digital technologies really is an addiction.

Today's society is highly dependent on digital technology, to the point that it is increasingly difficult—sometimes impossible—to buy things that do not contain some kind of computer. New cars, thermostats, credit cards, and other everyday items contain computer parts such as microchips. Global positioning systems (GPS) help people get to and from their destinations every day. Apps help keep track of subway schedules and warn commuters of possible delays. People work on personal computers and read on tablets and cell phones.

It makes sense to use digital technologies since life in industrialized countries is so dependent on them. It would be incredibly difficult for a person to function in society if they chose not to use any of them. However, is being dependent on technology the same thing as having an addiction?

Addiction and Dependency

The term "addiction" was first used in ancient Rome to describe a situation where a person owed money and was sentenced to slavery in order to pay off that debt. "It evolved to describe any bond that was difficult to break,"[7] explained Adam Alter in his book *Irresistible: The Rise of Addictive Technology and the Business of Keeping Us Hooked*. Addiction today means a person is mentally or physically bound to a substance or a behavior. An addiction is a chronic disease, and it affects the way the brain and body function.

Real addiction is a complicated brain disease. According to the American Society of Addiction Medicine, "Addiction is a primary, chronic disease of brain reward, motivation, memory and related circuitry."[8] Almost all medical associations believe addiction is a disease similar to diabetes or cancer. Just like other diseases, addiction is triggered by environmental factors as well as behavioral and genetic factors. As the Center on Addiction points out, the initial choice to use a substance or engage in a behavior is often of a person's own free will, but "once the brain has been changed by addiction, that choice or willpower becomes impaired."[9] Like other diseases, an addiction impairs the way the human body functions.

It is important to note that an addiction is not the same as a dependency. A person who has an addiction also generally has a physical or mental dependency, which means they do not feel normal either mentally or physically without the substance or activity. They have cravings and go to great lengths to get whatever they are addicted to, even when it is noticeably harming their health, career, or social life. In contrast, a dependency without an addiction is when the person needs the thing they are dependent on but does not crave it in the same way. For example, someone with type 1 diabetes is dependent on their insulin; they need it to stay alive, and if they do not get it, they will feel physically ill. However, it would be inaccurate to say that they are addicted to it since it is not activating the reward centers of their brain and using it every day does not negatively interfere with the rest of their life. Similarly, most people are dependent on technology in today's society. Someone without access to the internet loses out on job opportunities, connection to distant loved ones, and information that could be helpful to them. However, many people are able to put down their phones or computers and enjoy other activities without constantly thinking about the things they could be doing with their digital gadgets.

At least half a person's risk of developing an addiction to something can be linked to genes, which are the parts of deoxyribonucleic acid (DNA) that pass on certain traits from parent to child. Genes play a role in determining nearly all of a person's physical and personality traits, although experts disagree on how large that role is in some cases. Scientists have begun mapping the DNA of people with addictions to find patterns and identify gene variations that make a person more vulnerable. There is no single "addiction gene" that can be identified; instead, multiple factors play a role. For example, it has been shown that people with fewer D2 dopamine receptors in the brain are more likely to become addicted to substances such as alcohol, heroin, and cocaine during their lifetime. Dopamine is a neurotransmitter, or brain chemical, that has long been known to play a role in addiction because it activates the brain's reward and pleasure centers. Something that makes a person feel good—whether it is a food, drug, or activity—is causing the release of dopamine into the brain to achieve that good feeling. Receptors in the brain, such as D2 receptors (a specific type of dopamine receptor), are proteins that bind with the dopamine. The number of D2 receptors someone has is partially determined by genetics, which is why some people have a higher risk of addiction through no fault of their own. Because genes are passed down through families, if a person has a first-degree relative such as a parent or sibling who has an addiction, the probability of that individual developing an addiction is higher than it is for someone who does not have any family members with an addiction.

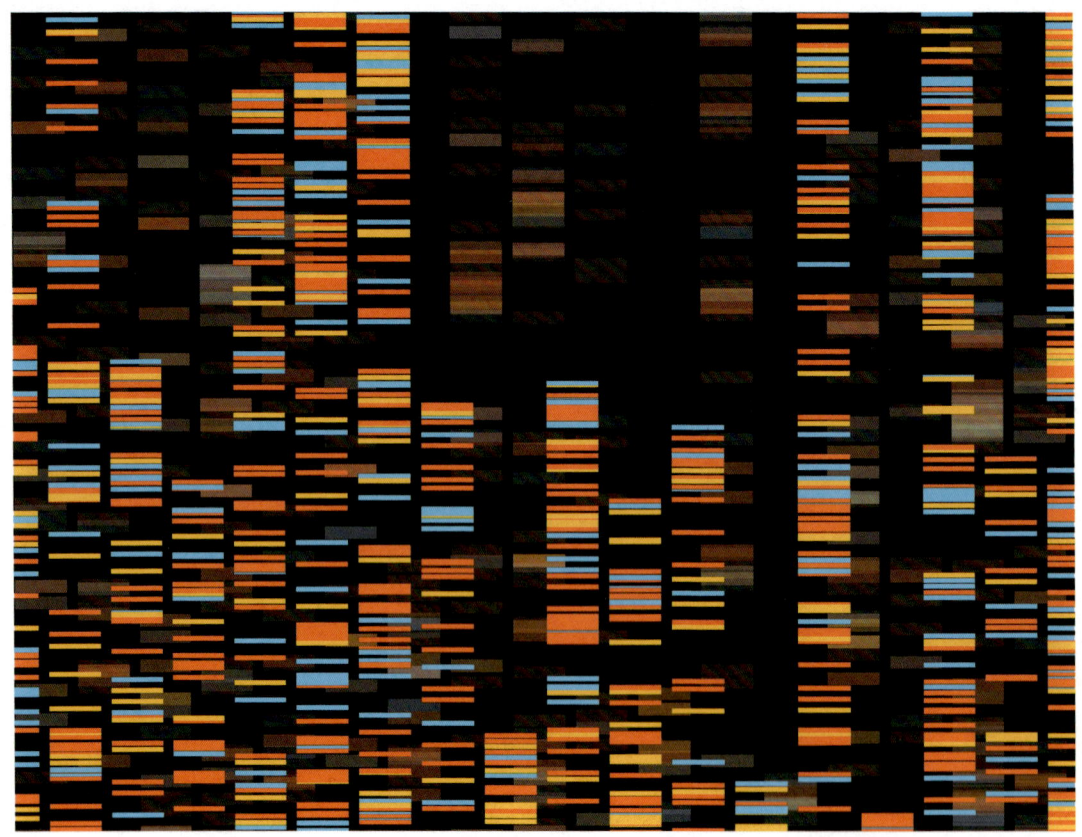

Data related to genes can be displayed as bars similar to those shown here.

The other major factor involved in the development of addictions is environment, or the conditions around a person. This includes with whom a person lives, where they work, the friends they have, and the community in which they live. For example, if a person does not have many friends in their community, they might turn to online chat rooms to make connections. This person is seeking to fill a need and might become dependent upon chat rooms and feel unconnected without them. If they start skipping work or not getting enough sleep so they can stay online chatting, they might be addicted to this behavior. Once the behavior has become an addiction, it can give the individual trouble developing relationships in person. Another example may be that an individual is extremely stressed at work and uses social media as a way of distracting themselves from the anxiety. Without the stressful environment, the individual may not have turned to social media as a way to feel better in the first place.

In fact, research has shown that environment plays a huge factor in whether or not someone develops an addiction. During the Vietnam War, for example, many soldiers were stuck waiting around for orders or combat. Out of

Between battles, Vietnam War soldiers spent long hours awaiting orders. In this environment, many turned to heroin and became addicted.

boredom, many of them experimented with heroin. Research has shown that 35 percent of the people who served in Vietnam tried heroin, and 20 percent of those who used it were addicted to it. When these numbers were discovered, President Richard Nixon worked with his staff to create the Special Action Office of Drug Abuse Prevention, which followed up with service members after they returned home. Their findings revealed that approximately nine out of ten soldiers overcame their heroin addiction right away, and the reason for the change was entirely to do with environment. In their homes and communities, the returning soldiers were less likely to feel the boredom, stress, and isolation they felt while serving in Vietnam and therefore less likely to crave heroin as a way to alter their emotions and mental state.

For many people with an addiction, rehabilitation centers—frequently shortened simply to "rehab"—are a key component for overcoming the addiction, or "getting clean." Once they are away from the environment that prompted them to start using drugs in the first place, they have an easier time stopping their substance use. However, when patients leave rehab and return to their previous environment, many of them revert back to their addictions. An article by Bobby P. Smyth in the *Irish Medical Journal* found that 91 percent of heroin users become readdicted after returning home from rehab. This is not because these people have no willpower but because they are returning to an environment that led them to addiction in the first place.

In fact, one of the most misunderstood parts about addiction is that it is considered a moral failing. Society most often views a person who is addicted to a substance or a behavior as having a lack of self-control or being a bad person. According to author James Clear, who writes about the ways habits affect behavior, "The people with the best self-control are typically the ones who need to use it the least. It's easier to practice self-restraint when you don't have to use it very often."[10] Basically, when put into the right circumstances, a lot of people would be tempted. The best defense against addiction is not being tempted in the first place, but for

What Is an Addiction?

many people, the circumstances that tempt them are beyond their control.

In order to properly and effectively address addiction, the cultural understanding of it needs to shift. Someone with an addiction is not a failure; they have simply been placed in an environment that has made it easier to develop a disease. Society needs to work to ensure that people are not placed in circumstances that would make them fall victim to addiction. Many people ask, "Is someone with an

When needs are met by people's communities, they are less likely to become addicted to digital technologies.

addiction bad?" However, a more useful question is, "How can environments and lifestyles be designed in order for people to live at their best?"

Behavioral Addictions

When people think about addictions, they generally think of substance addictions—the overuse of alcohol or drugs. However, people frequently become addicted to behaviors as well. Behavioral addictions are also sometimes called process addictions.

NOT A TRUE ADDICTION?

"Addiction doesn't really capture the behavior we're seeing ... With addiction, you have a chemical that changes the way we respond, that leads us to be reliant on it for our level of functioning. That's not what's happening here. We don't develop higher levels of tolerance. We don't need more and more screen time in order to be able to function."

–Dr. Matthew Cruger, neuropsychologist and director of the Learning and Development Center at the Child Mind Institute

Quoted in Caroline Miller, "Is Internet Addiction Real?," Child Mind Institute, accessed on January 23, 2019. childmind.org/article/is-internet-addiction-real/

Some people believe it is impossible to get addicted to something without altering the body by a synthetic chemical reaction. This means they think someone must take something into the body, such as a drug, that forces a chemical change to happen in the brain. In some fundamental ways, substance addiction and behavioral addiction are different because of this fact. However, using brain imaging techniques, scientists have discovered that the same areas of the brain become active whether the addiction involves a substance or a behavior.

Other studies have found that behavioral addictions are far from rare. In 2011, a review paper published by psychology professor Mark Griffiths and two researchers from the University of Southern California found that about 41 percent of the world's population had experienced at least one behavioral addiction over the previous 12 months. To reach this conclusion, the researchers reviewed previously published studies that were only included in the project "if they had at least five hundred respondents, both men and women, aged between sixteen and sixty-five years, and their measurement methods had to be reliable and supported with careful research."[11] Anything that did not meet these criteria was less likely to be applicable to the general population. Overall, the three researchers reviewed 83 studies that included a total of 1.5 million respondents from four different continents.

Digital addictions are behavioral addictions. The repetition of certain behaviors, such as engaging in a video game or scrolling through social media, actually cause chemical reactions in the brain even though no outside chemicals are being ingested. Doctors Jon E. Grant, Brian L. Odlaug, and Samuel R. Chamberlain say that digital addictions can be just as damaging as drug addictions. They wrote, "The reinforcement of the behaviors can be so strong that some people go through withdrawal when they stop the behavior, just as in drug and alcohol addiction."[12]

Fortunately, with the right training, it is possible for people to learn how to set healthy boundaries around their digital usage. This is an important skill to learn because digital technologies are not going away. Jessica Wong, a state-certified prevention professional at the Hazelden Betty Ford Foundation in St. Paul, Minnesota, stressed that with a plan set in place, most people can overcome their addiction to digital technologies.

Addictions are known to affect the mesolimbic dopamine pathway, which is sometimes known as the reward circuit. The mesolimbic pathway includes multiple parts of the brain. Information travels from the ventral tegmental area (VTA), which is located near the brain stem, to the nucleus accumbens and then through to the prefrontal cortex at the front of the head. Communication in the brain is called neurotransmission. Anytime the brain receives information from other parts of the body—when the eyes read text, when the fingers touch something hot, when the tongue tastes something sweet—this information is processed. Neurotransmitters bind with receptors, which send the neuron a signal to fire, sending an electrical signal to the axon, the part of the nerve that sends the signal to the appropriate part of the body. Once that happens, the brain processes the information and reacts to it.

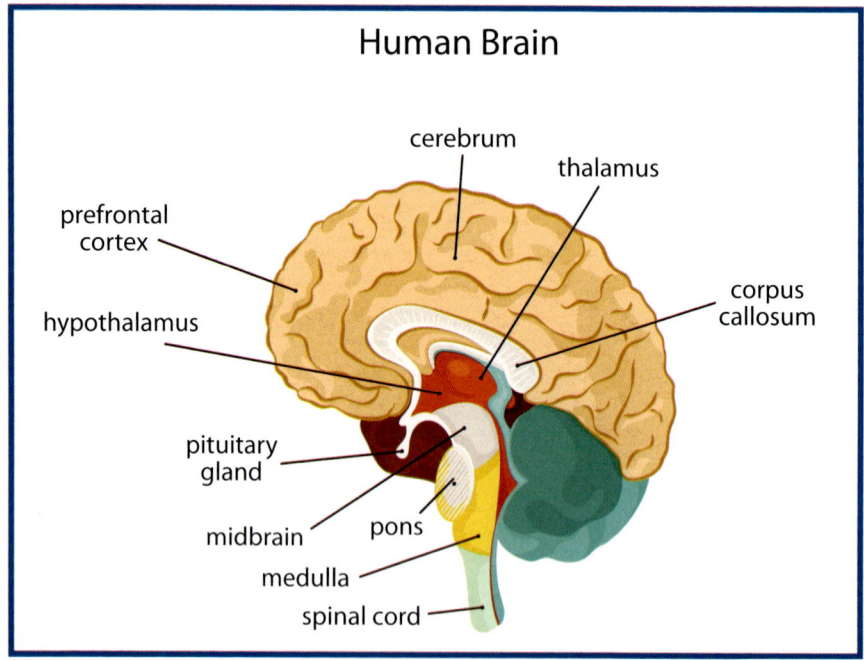

The brain is a complex organ, and all the parts work together to keep the body functioning correctly. When the brain is affected by an addiction, so is the body.

Addictions disrupt the normal process of neurotransmission. This results in a buildup of neurotransmitters, which causes the neurons to fire continuously as they are stimulated by the receptors. This may account for the high some drugs or behaviors cause. It was originally thought that dopamine caused the sensation of pleasure, but now scientists know that dopamine is released even before an event happens: The anticipation of an event that someone associates with good feelings can spike dopamine levels.

Behaviors do not physically affect neurotransmission exactly the same way a substance does, so researchers are still trying to understand why people with behavioral addictions have similar reactions without the stimulus of chemical substances. There is a lot about the brain experts still do not know, but the technology needed for effective brain research is improving, so researchers are hopeful that someday the mysteries of the brain will be solved.

As of 2019, digital addiction is not listed in the *Diagnostic and Statistical Manual of Mental Disorders* (*DSM*), which is the book mental health experts use to diagnose mental disorders. Originally published in 1952, the *DSM* is now in its fifth edition; it is updated occasionally to reflect new research, so some disorders may be added, removed, or reclassified over time. Some people hope digital addiction will be added to the next revision, because along with each diagnosis, the book lists codes that are used to bill health insurance companies. As long as digital addiction is not listed in the *DSM*, patients have to pay out of pocket for any treatment options, which can be very expensive.

There is a push to include more behavioral addictions, including digital addiction, in the next edition of the *DSM*.

IN THE DSM

"It takes years of research to establish new disorders. Just look how long substance dependence—such as alcoholism—or pathological gambling or eating disorders took to get into the DSM. Plus all the research done on Internet addiction used a variety of methods and measurements, so it was unclear if we were all studying the same phenomenon."

–Dr. Kimberley Young, internet addiction therapist

Quoted in David McNamee, "Technology Addiction: How Should It Be Treated?," *Medical News Today*, September 1, 2015. www.medicalnewstoday.com/articles/278530.php.

The problem researchers have is that it is difficult to know whether a behavioral addiction is an actual disease in and of itself or if it is a symptom of an underlying disorder, such as obsessive-compulsive disorder (OCD) or attention-deficit/hyperactivity disorder (ADHD). Research has linked digital addiction with many underlying issues, but it is hard to tell without further research whether they are related or not. People who have mental illnesses frequently have more than one; when two diseases appear together but are not necessarily caused by each other, they are called comorbidities. For example, clinical depression is frequently comorbid with anxiety disorders, but while anxiety can make depression worse, it does not necessarily cause it. There is still a lot of research to be done, but since there is evidence that behavioral addictions are similar to substance addictions, it is important to develop the mindset of treating behavioral addiction the same way a substance addiction would be treated. Even if digital addictions are not diagnosable by the *DSM*, they still take a toll on individuals who suffer from them.

In 2018, the World Health Organization (WHO) published the 11th International Classification of Diseases (ICD), which did include "gaming disorder." This describes an addiction to video or computer games in which someone ignores important tasks as well as previous interests, such as spending time with friends, in favor of playing games. According to WHO, "For gaming disorder to be diagnosed, the behavior pattern must be of sufficient severity to result in significant impairment in personal, family, social, educational, occupational or other important areas of functioning and would normally have been evident for at least 12 months."[13] According to Dr. Richard Graham of the Nightingale Hospital in London, England, officially defining this disorder "is significant because it creates the opportunity for more specialised services. It puts it on the map as something to take seriously."[14]

Distracted Parenting

Many people are concerned about the effects of digital technologies on children and teens in particular. Robert Lustig, a professor of pediatrics whose focus is on endocrinology (the study of hormones) at the University of California, San Francisco, says adolescents are especially susceptible to addictions of any type because the prefrontal cortex is the last part of the brain to develop. The human brain does not stop developing until someone is in their late 20s or early 30s. However, many experts point out that the way children are raised has a great deal to do with someone's potential addiction risk.

In an article for *The Atlantic*, writer Erika Christakis noted that because of the increasing availability of screens, parents today have less quality time with their children. When parents are distracted by their devices, it can be difficult for children to become socialized because they may not receive the traditional responses to their attempts at communication. Research has also shown that children learn better from real people than from videos, so children whose parents do not talk to them much may have a harder time learning language. This can impact their future school grades. According to Kathy Hirsh-Pasek, a professor at Temple University and a senior fellow at the Brookings Institute, "Toddlers cannot learn when we break the flow of our conversations by picking up our cellphones or looking at the text that whizzes by our screens."[1] Parents cannot pay constant attention to their children, so some interruption is expected, but a problem arises when parents are constantly distracted. In addition to affecting the way children learn, this type of behavior generally serves as a model for the child, who may be more likely to constantly be distracted by their own devices in the future.

1. Quoted in Erika Christakis, "The Dangers of Distracted Parenting," *The Atlantic*, July/August 2018. www.theatlantic.com/magazine/archive/2018/07/the-dangers-of-distracted-parenting/561752/.

Skeptics

On the other end of the spectrum, there are many people, including some experts, who do not believe digital addiction is a true problem. While the media tends to portray it as an increasing epidemic, causing many people to view technology use with concern, some scientists argue that just the release of dopamine as a result of engaging in a behavior does not mean someone is getting high. In fact, many things trigger dopamine responses, such as exercise and certain foods. Dopamine is a normal and necessary neurotransmitter; too little of it can cause depression. To some experts, the comparison of technology to cocaine or heroin is frustrating. As Dr. Amy Orben pointed out, "If we have people who are seen as experts telling parents that giving their child a smartphone, which is a daily object of use, is like giving them a gram of cocaine it's causing unnecessary concern in people who are already concerned."[15] Researcher danah boyd, who has spent years studying the ways young adults engage with technology, agrees that many people are too quick to call teens' online behavior an addiction. She noted that contrary to adults' fears that technology is making young adults less social, most of them use texting and social media to interact with their friends—just as past generations used to send letters through the mail or call each other on the phone just to chat. Teens who had more time to spend with their friends in person tended to use social media less, she found.

Overreacting to normal, harmless digital behavior, many argue, can have other bad consequences. Professor Andrew Przybylski believes that the conversation about how tech affects the brain takes the spotlight off more pressing questions, such as who has access to people's data and how they are using it. "If we're so busy being the boy who cried wolf," he said, "we're not actually going to get any better [at] detecting wolves."[16]

Not Enough Research

As author Anya Kamenetz pointed out in her book *The Art of Screen Time*, researching the effects of digital technologies is problematic for many reasons, the first and foremost being that there is no control group for any scientific study. There are not many people who use no technology at all, and it is hard to make comparisons to the ones who exist, such as certain Amish populations or people who choose to live off the grid, because their lifestyle is so vastly different from the mainstream. While there are tests where people choose not to use digital technologies for a short period of time, such as a week or a month, the number of people who do it is too small and the length of time is too short for researchers to make solid comparisons. In addition, not a lot of time has gone by since digital technologies became so common in everyday life. Because of that, it is impossible to talk about long-term effects with any sort of clarity.

Technology Taking Over

As humans increasingly depend upon technologies, they will become even more a part of daily life. Already, people use digital technologies a lot. Many people in 2019 use their mobile devices to conduct internet banking, make purchases, and communicate with people all over the world. Online-only money called bitcoin has gained popularity in recent years. Without a doubt, in 20 or 30 years, the digital landscape will look much different than it does today.

Humans are very social creatures and often develop patterns by observing social behavior and engaging in the same things they see others doing. In evolutionary terms, social behavior is very useful. Loners tend not to live as long as creatures in a tight-knit pack because there is safety in numbers. Biologically, humans want to be alike—but only up to a point. Most humans also want to be seen as unique.

Human instincts greatly influence digital technologies. They are designed to be useable—and often, digital technologies are almost too easy to use. It is easy to become hooked on tech, and when more and more people engage in the behavior, it becomes easier to justify that behavior, even when it gets out of hand.

A Digital Environment

One of the biggest problems in the digital age is that people's everyday environment is set up in a way that it makes it easy for them to become addicted. Billions of dollars are spent in

Technology Taking Over 41

Digital devices, with their sleek designs, are developed to be used intuitively, or instinctively.

the technology industry to figure out how to make people spend as much time as possible using digital devices.

Some people argue that addiction to technology is less a mental problem and more a socioeconomic problem. Technology companies make a lot of profit, and these corporations are fighting each other for the money and time of their users. Video game developers, social media companies, and technology innovators all employ hundreds of people to make sure their products are appealing to consumers. By charging for apps, getting companies to pay for ads on free games, and convincing people to buy the latest products, technology is a financially rewarding business. In 2017, Apple was named the most profitable company for the third year in a row by *Fortune* magazine. The previous year, the company had made $45.7 billion in profit.

As these corporations have gained more power over consumers—for example, creating ads targeted toward each specific person based on things such as their search history—some people believe they should be regulated to protect individuals. Adam Alter argued that the environment of the digital age is a breeding ground for addictions. He wrote, "Users benefit from these apps and websites, but also struggle to use them in moderation."[17]

Many people all over the world use their mobile devices and computers to make payments.

Fear of Technology

According to the Survey of American Fears released by researchers at California's Chapman University in 2015, one of the top five fears Americans have is the fear of technology. "People tend to express the highest level of fear for things they're dependent on but that they have no control over, and that's almost a perfect definition of technology,"[18] explained Christopher Bader, a professor of sociology and one of the coauthors of the study. The use of technology is controversial, and because many people fear technology, its use is often viewed negatively. A person who does not like technology may see normal use as excessive use.

Indeed, new technologies have always been looked at with skepticism. Swiss scientist Conrad Gessner preached in the mid-1500s that an overabundance of information was both "confusing and harmful"[19] to the mind. These words were in response to the printing press, which was new technology at the time. When radios became available for household use, they were also met with concern; some people worried that children would become distracted by the radio and pay less attention to their homework. They had the same concerns about movies, and then later about television. Even today, there are many concerns about watching too much television. Apart from worrying about the effect television, like other screens, has on the mind, experts have seen a disturbing rise in obesity in the 21st century, which some people have attributed to too much time spent sitting and watching TV. For example, Dr. Dennis Rosen wrote in *Psychology Today* in 2009, "The more TV you watch, the fatter you become."[20]

This sedentary, or inactive, lifestyle is something people worry about with smartphones and computers as well. Authors Joe Clement and Matt Miles argue that smartphone use is more problematic than television viewing. In their book *Screen Schooled: Two Veteran Teachers Expose How Technology Overuse Is Making Our Kids Dumber*, they wrote, "Especially early on, television and television shows were (and in many cases still are) events. Families and friends gathered to experience shows together. More important, televisions were in the living room, and they stayed there."[21] Digital technologies, instead, travel with people and are easier to use all the time. In 2017, the *New York Post* reported that based on research conducted by a global tech protection and support company called Asurion, Americans check their phones

In the early days of television, with only a handful of channels, watching programming was often a family affair.

about once every 12 minutes. The availability of technology makes it easier to form an addiction. When something is always around, it becomes easier to indulge in it compared to something a person would have to seek out or buy. It can also make other addictions worse. For example, before the internet was common in people's homes, someone with a shopping addiction would only be able to shop when the stores were open. Today, someone could spend all their money on shopping without even leaving the house.

The digital landscape has created the perfect environment for people to become addicted—and one of the biggest problems is that it is a for-profit industry. For example, the online game *League of Legends* makes $1.6 billion per year. From a business point of view, it makes sense that the people behind the game would want to ensure that players become addicted and stay addicted, since the more they play, the more money the creators make. Alter argued that so many people are addicted to technology not because they lack willpower, but because the systems are designed by experts to keep people hooked.

Designing an Addictive Experience

Many people find themselves staying online longer than they intended. They may start scrolling through social media feeds as a five-minute break from work, but then all of a sudden realize that an hour has passed. Digital corporations have a team of designers that work to attract users' attention in exactly this way.

Multiple things contribute to creating an addictive experience. For example, whenever a notification comes in, a person experiences a rush of dopamine to the brain. The notification has interrupted whatever else was going on, and often, the phone buzzes to get the user's attention. These notifications can give a rush of excitement that feels similar to gambling: It could be that someone has sent a friend request, that someone has liked a post, or that an app is giving a call to action, such as Facebook informing the user that a friend is interested in going to an event nearby. The notification could be anything, and the temptation to check and see what kind of "prize" has been "won" can be irresistable. People tend to keep their phones on them in case they miss a notification and therefore miss out on something important. This is so common that "fear of missing out" has been shortened to FOMO.

> ## GETTING AWAY FROM FOMO
>
> "What you attend to drives your behavior and it determines your happiness. Attention is the glue that holds your life together ... So changing behavior and enhancing happiness is as much about withdrawing attention from the negative as it is about attending to the positive."
>
> —Paul Dolan, author of *Happiness By Design: Change What You Do, Not How You Think*

Quoted in Eric Barker, "This Is The Best Way to Overcome Fear of Missing Out," *TIME*, June 7, 2016. time.com/4358140/overcome-fomo/.

Studies have shown that it takes about 23 minutes for a person to get back on track mentally after being distracted. Even having a phone in the same general area can be distracting. Although the user may have chosen not to actively engage with the device, they may be consciously or unconsciously listening for the sounds of a notification.

Another thing that keeps people checking their phones is the prospect of getting an ego boost. Social media companies know that approval can be a very motivating force. Social approval happens when someone likes something that someone else has put online. The person who posted feels as if they have done something correct and that they are well-liked. Most people depend on others' approval to some degree to create a good self-image. Taking advantage of this basic human need, social media designers often make posts more visible when they get more approval. For example, a profile picture change that has many likes is often seen by many people as followers continue to like it. The more likes or upvotes a post has, the more frequently it is seen.

Other online companies use human instinct as well. Many video streaming websites, such as YouTube and Netflix, have an autoplay feature, where the next episode in a series or a video similar to the one that was just watched automatically plays after a countdown. If someone is not paying attention to the countdown, they may get invested in the video once it starts and find it hard to stop watching, even if they only meant to watch one thing. In contrast to shows that air on cable television once a week, multiple episodes of series are available all at once on services such as Netflix and Hulu. Because of this, the term "binge-watching" was coined to describe the increasingly common situation in which someone watches multiple episodes of a show in a short period of time.

Other digital technologies focus on social reciprocity, meaning a person feels an obligation to return a favor. In an article for *Story Bistro*, Téa Silvestre Godfrey talked about the concept of #FollowFriday, or #FF. This started on social media platforms such as Instagram as a way for people to help others gain followers. However, Godfrey noted, some people see #FF as an obligation. She wrote,

> *I'd posted a link to my Word Chef fan page and then proceeded to like only the pages that I felt were relevant to my interests ... I wound up getting private messages from several of the admins of those pages that I hadn't liked—usually indignant reminders that they had liked my page and therefore deserved to have me like them back ... Reciprocity has been taken too dang far. Just because someone likes or follows you doesn't mean you're obligated to auto-like or follow them back. In fact, I think that doing things like that is a terrible waste of time and energy ... That's not how we create deep, meaningful relationships.*[22]

Feeling obligated to return advances on social media can cause someone to spend a lot of time checking their notifications and worrying about what the "correct" time frame is for following or liking someone else's social media.

The design of social media platforms is based on social reciprocity, so if many people like a post, the poster often spends more time online returning the favor.

Digital technologies are naturally habit-forming because they are so widely available and easy to use. Once a person gets in the habit of checking their social media feed or playing a game every day, it becomes easier and easier to keep doing it. While a habit can turn into an addiction, Jessica Wong explained that "it takes a lot for technology use to meet the definition of dependence. We call it addiction when it starts to impact day-to-day function, relationships with children, spouses … and friends."[23]

Digital Devices: The Good

The brain processes all the information a person receives through the five senses, and the brain changes based on what it receives. According to Bryan Kolb, an expert in brain development, "Experience alters brain activity, which changes gene expression [which genes are active]. Any behavioral changes you see reflect alterations in the brain. The opposite is also true: behavior can change the brain."[24] One of the best-known studies on this phenomenon took place in 2000. In London, England, taxi drivers must memorize the streets of the city and pass a memory test before they can get their license. This ensures that they do not get lost and overcharge their customers by taking an inefficient route. In the study, London taxi drivers were given brain scans, and the results showed that the ones who had been doing the work the longest had visible changes in brain structure. Most notably, they had larger hippocampuses because they were exercising that area of the brain, which is involved in storing and retrieving memories, every day. Knowing that the brain changes based on environmental information, it is clear that screen-based technology will contribute to those changes. However, experts disagree on whether the change is beneficial or not, as well as exactly what types of changes will take place over time.

There are noted benefits to screen time. Many scientists believe digital technology improves certain kinds of learning. For example, according to Susan Greenfield, playing video games can improve the ways people react to input from their senses as well as the ways they learn to react to that same input in the future. Studies show that programs that attempt to increase the brain's processing speed have promise. As the brain works in these programs, it forms new neural pathways—an ability called neuroplasticity—to help people recall their new skills more easily. People who have used these types of training programs have reported feeling sharper in everyday life—for instance, better able to recall what a friend said or a fact they recently learned. However, it is not enough for

Digital Dependency

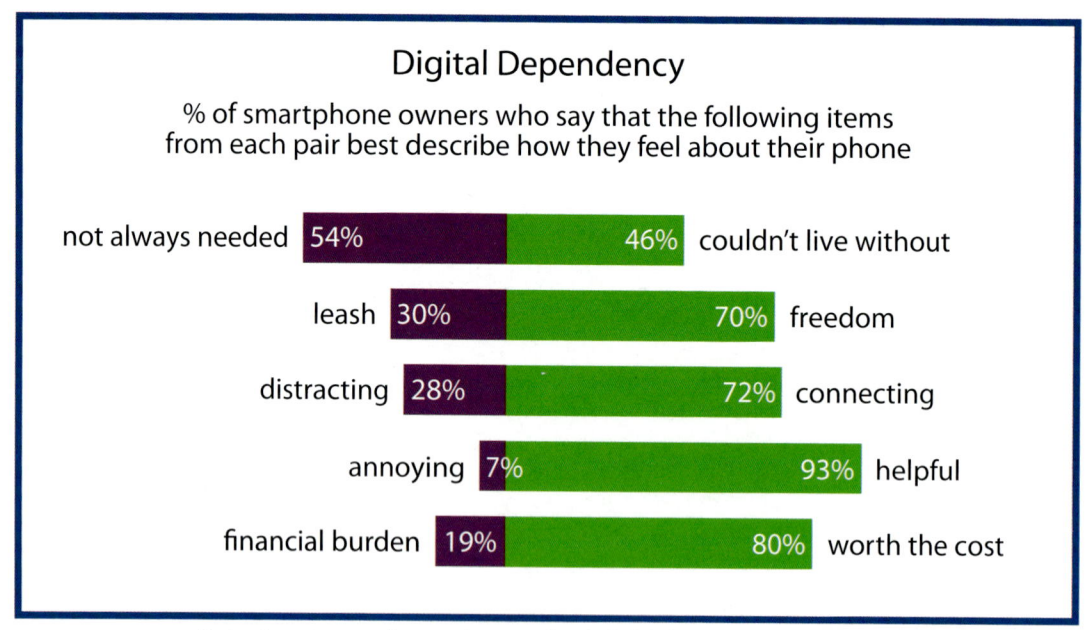

% of smartphone owners who say that the following items from each pair best describe how they feel about their phone

not always needed	54% / 46%	couldn't live without
leash	30% / 70%	freedom
distracting	28% / 72%	connecting
annoying	7% / 93%	helpful
financial burden	19% / 80%	worth the cost

Technology is more frequently viewed as helpful than as harmful, as this information from the Pew Research Center shows.

these programs to be digital; they must also be well-designed. Other mind-training apps that claim to improve brain function have failed in clinical testing. One study done at the University of Pennsylvania showed that Lumosity, a memory and attention game, did not have any effect on cognitive performance. The company was fined $2 million for deceptive advertising.

Author Clive Thompson believes that if digital technologies are used in a smart way, they can make humans smarter, just as certain non-digital tools and practices do. While doing research for his book *Smarter Than You Think: How Technology Is Changing Our Brains for the Better*, Thompson interviewed individuals who have used digital technologies for many years. A man named Gordon Bell, for example, has been using portable digital technology for years. He wears an eyepiece that takes pictures every 60 seconds and an audio recorder that captures conversations. In this way, Bell can search his records for any person or topic he has encountered since he began wearing the digital devices. According to Bell, having this information has given him mental peace and allows him to live fully in each moment. He can keep track of all of his conversations and ideas; if he cannot remember something exactly, he can easily look it up. He does not consider this reliance on technology to be an addiction because, he said, he only does this to aid conversations; he does not surf the web while doing other activities or speaking directly to someone. While he has gained a lot from this experiment, there have

Shown here is Khee Lee of Google wearing Google Glass, a portable digital device that allows a user to be connected at all times. While some people were interested in this device, it was too expensive and too limited to catch on.

also been some difficulties.

One of the biggest problems Bell says he has encountered is that searching for things is very difficult. With a catalog of all his daily conversations and events, there is much more information than he needs, and searching through it takes time. Additionally, the human brain quickly jumps from topic to topic, so his files are not organized. However, Thompson argued, when humans and technology use their complementary skills, people can do a lot more with the information they have access to.

That is the theory behind using technology in education today. Many schools give students tablets and laptops to use for taking notes and completing classwork. Some teachers believe digital technologies make teaching and learning more effective. Kami Thordarson, a teacher at Santa Rita Elementary in Los Altos, California, found that digital technology was able to help her teach multiple students who were all at different learning levels without ignoring any of them. The students use Khan Academy, an online platform that has video lessons that are about 10 to 15 minutes long. Students are able to go at their own pace when they do these lessons, and Thordarson is able to give individualized attention to students who need help. Some of the students are very advanced, doing work that is well above their actual grade level. Others struggle to learn, which is why Thordarson's job has not been completely replaced by digital technology. She noted that when she was lecturing without using digital technology, she was only teaching to about half of the class: One quarter of the class fell behind, while another quarter stopped paying attention because they already understood the concepts.

There are other ways technology can be helpful in the classroom. In 2015, for example, 350 students in professor Ashok Goel's Georgia Tech online course "Knowledge-Based Artificial Intelligence" posted 10,000 messages on the discussion forum. Professor Goel guessed that it would take a full-time working teacher a year to answer all the messages by themselves. Using data from previous semesters, Goel and two graduate students constructed an AI teaching assistant they named Jill Watson. After an initial run, Jill was allowed to answer questions on the forum. While there were a few errors, most students could not tell the difference between Jill and one of the living teaching assistants. The point of the exercise was to judge whether it was possible to use AI to free up some of the time humans would otherwise waste on repetitive tasks. By creating Jill, Goel was able to focus on the more creative aspects of the course instead of responding to each and every question—many of which were repeated by multiple students.

Many schools encourage the use of technology in the classroom.

Digital Technologies: The Bad

Other people are skeptical about giving digital technologies a more prominent spot in the classroom. Joe Clement and Matt Miles, who have been teachers for many years, see more screen time in the classroom as a negative. They have seen kids becoming distracted, and they have seen what they describe as a decline in the classroom. Clement and Miles do not believe screens help students, and they have concerns about schools pushing more screen time on them. Partially, they believe, this is because companies are partnering with schools to sell more digital technologies. Indeed, Google has made a concentrated effort to get more of its products into the classroom by offering low-cost devices and free apps such as Google Classroom, which is meant to help students and teachers share paperless documents with each other. The app includes Google Docs, Google Calendar, Google Drive, and more. Because of its efforts, Google has dominated the education market and gotten its devices and programming into the hands of more than 30 million children in the United States.

While it may seem as though Google is being generous, Natasha Singer pointed out in an article in the *New York Times* that Google may be getting a lot more than it is giving. When students graduate after using Google Classroom, they are already used to using Google software. It makes sense for many of them to transition to private Google accounts and continue to use Google products. In addition, Google already knows a lot about each student. Some people have concerns about the kinds of information Google collects and what it does with that information. Indeed, privacy issues revolving around technology are a major concern, and many people have called for tech companies to be more open about how they use the data they collect.

Singer also pointed out that the digitalization of American classrooms is changing how children are educated. She wrote,

> Google is helping to drive a philosophical change in public education—prioritizing training children in skills like teamwork and problem-solving while de-emphasizing the teaching of

traditional academic knowledge, like math formulas. It puts Google, and the tech economy, at the center of one of the great debates that has raged in American education for more than a century: whether the purpose of public schools is to turn out knowledgeable citizens or skilled workers.[25]

Many people believe it is important to consider what is better for society and not allow a corporation to dictate the education system—or any other system. When people are better informed, they can make better choices.

Some people believe Google should be more transparent about the information it collects from students and how that information is used.

Effects on the Brain

One important thing researchers are concerned about is how technology is affecting social development. Because kids and teens interact frequently through texts and social media, some people fear they are not learning necessary social skills such as empathy, or the ability to understand and relate to someone else's feelings. As Dr. Michele Borba explained, "It's very hard to be empathetic and feel for another human being if you can't read another person's emotions. You don't learn emotional literacy facing a screen. You don't learn emotional literacy with emojis."[26] Social cues take a long time to learn, and it is only through repeated exposure in different circumstances that those skills are really cemented. In fact, researchers have discovered kids now may be less empathetic than kids in earlier decades, who grew up without digital technologies.

However, others believe this fear is blown out of proportion. They point out that empathy is a natural human ability that most people have, and while practice can improve it, lack of practice does not necessarily mean someone is completely lacking empathy. They also argue that human empathy has natural limits, so technology may not be causing less empathy, only highlighting the point at which empathy naturally declines. For example, in an article on *The Cut*, writer Jesse Singal discussed crowdfunding for medical bills through websites such as GoFundMe. This has become a common practice in the United States, where health insurance has severe limitations and many people end up with large medical bills they cannot pay. The article noted that "it's generally easy to crowdfund for so-called 'faultless' conditions like cancer and genetic disorders as compared to conditions like 'addiction and mental health in particular' which society generally views as the result of bad decision making or some sort of moral shortcoming."[27] This is caused by attitudes that are reinforced in multiple areas of society, but it is more easily noticed when certain people's online crowdfunding is ignored.

Another concern researchers have is the effect of technology on attention spans. One study from South Korea showed that teenagers with smartphone addictions had higher levels of a neurotransmitter called gamma aminobutyric acid (GABA) that slows down neurons. The result was that these teenagers had less of an ability to concentrate. According to a press release by the Radiological Society of North America, "Having too much GABA can result in a number of side effects, including drowsiness and anxiety,"[28] both of which can impair a person's concentration. The study found that

Researchers have learned that reading body language—a skill that generally cannot be learned from digital devices—is crucial to the development of important human social traits, such as empathy.

neurotransmitters leveled out once the addicted teenagers went through cognitive behavioral therapy (CBT). However,

Violence and Video Games

Many people argue that violent video games make players more violent and antisocial. By using studies that pulled from laboratory research and following online gamers, the American Psychological Association (APA) concluded in 2015 that violent video games do make it more difficult for people to have empathy with other people. However, other studies have shown that there is no conclusive link. *Scientific American* noted several limitations of the APA's research; for instance, "lab studies measure aggressiveness by offering participants the chance to inflict a punishment, such as a dose of very hot sauce to swallow—actions that are hardly representative of real life. Outside the lab, participants would probably give more consideration to the harmful nature of their actions."[1] It is difficult to say whether violent video games make people more violent or if people who are more predisposed to violence play violent video games.

There have been multiple reports of violence in connection with gaming. For example, a woman named Barbara McVeigh described her nine-year-old son's digital use as it took a scary turn, explaining, "He would refuse to do anything unless I would let him play his game."[2] Her son became increasingly violent, and when McVeigh tried to take the computer away, he attacked her.

Critics point out that this is an extreme case and that millions of people play video games—even violent ones—without committing actual violence. They also note that some people who commit violent acts do not play video games at all. Still, it is important for people to be aware of the power of media influence and how digital devices fit into the picture.

1. Elena Pasquinelli, "Are Digital Devices Altering Our Brains?," *Scientific American*, September 11, 2018. www.scientificamerican.com/article/are-digital-devices-altering-our-brains/.
2. Quoted in Nicholas Kardaras, "Kids Turn Violent as Parents Battle 'Digital Heroin' Addiction," *New York Post*, December 17, 2016. nypost.com/2016/12/17/kids-turn-violent-as-parents-battle-digital-heroin-addiction/.

more research must be done to confirm these findings, as experts are still unsure if the imbalance was caused by screens or if it happened first and caused the teens to become addicted to technology.

This is the greatest challenge of deciding whether digital technologies are good or bad for the brain, or even if they have any noticeable effect at all: Scientists simply do not know enough about the brain. Part of the problem is that the brain is very complex, and in order to understand it better, scientists must approach research from multiple perspectives. After all, technology is not the only thing people encounter on a daily basis, so scientists want to know how the brain takes in sensory information and how it reacts to that information. Research is being done, but it will be years before scientists fully understand how the brain works. Until that point, based on the currently available research, the American Academy of Pediatrics (AAP) has recommended that screen time should not be allowed for children younger than 18 months old and should be limited to one hour per day for children between the ages of 2 and 5. For young people older than this, parents are advised to set their own limits that they feel work best for their family.

SCREENS DO NOT CHANGE PERSONALITIES

"It is easy to blame social media ... since much research finds that narcissistic people use social media more frequently and for more self-promoting reasons ... But this doesn't mean that social media always creates narcissism—it is likely that offline narcissists are also online narcissists."

—Sara Konrath, assistant professor at the Institute for Social Research at the University of Michigan

Sara Konrath, "Is Declining Empathy Technology's Fault?," *New York Times*, September 23, 2013. www.nytimes.com/roomfordebate/2013/09/23/facebook-and-narcissism/is-declining-empathy-technologys-fault.

Lack of Sleep

Although there are many uncertainties about how technology is affecting people, researchers do know that it is impacting the amount and quality of many people's sleep. This is a major issue because sleep, in turn, affects all areas of a person's life, including their mental and physical health. It also affects performance at work and school.

Sleep is very important; a good night's sleep is needed for the body to repair muscles, adequately process memories, and release the proper hormones in the proper amounts to regulate the body. Not getting a good night's sleep consistently puts people at risk for physical health conditions such as obesity, heart disease, and diabetes, as well as mental health disorders such as depression and anxiety.

> ### SUCCESS AND SLEEP
>
> "I learned the hard way that there is no trade-off between living a well-rounded life and high performance—performance is actually improved when our lives include time for renewal. My advice to anyone putting life before sleep is this: you have an opportunity to immediately improve your health, creativity, productivity and sense of well-being. Start by getting just 30 minutes more sleep than you are getting now."
>
> –Arianna Huffington, founder of the *Huffington Post*
>
> Quoted in "Arianna Huffington Stresses the Importance of a Good Night's Sleep," Media Planet, accessed on December 26, 2018. www.futureofpersonalhealth.com/advocacy/arianna-huffington-stresses-the-importance-of-a-good-nights-sleep.

One of the most obvious ways technology can decrease sleep is that people frequently lose track of time while they are using their devices and stay up later than they intended to. For example, a person may start looking through their social media feeds as a way to unwind at night, but in truth, this activity can often keep them scrolling hours after they wanted to go to bed.

However, another problem is that digital screens give off a blue light, and when that light hits the eyes, the body stops producing the hormone melatonin. Melatonin is important because it regulates the circadian rhythm, or sleep cycle—when humans sleep and wake. Changes in melatonin levels can negatively affect sleep. People who use digital devices just before sleeping have a harder time falling asleep and staying asleep. According to Sleep.org, 39 percent of Americans bring their mobile devices to bed with them, so this problem is a common one—but people may not realize why they do not feel rested in the morning.

Many experts warn against using digital devices in bed as a way to relax before falling asleep because it often has the opposite effect.

There are some apps—such as f.lux, Twilight, and Night Shift—that put a red or orange filter on the device's screen after a certain time of the day to make the light less blue. While these apps can help, they are not a permanent solution for sleep loss since any type of light can have a negative effect on sleep. Many experts recommend setting limits on light-emitting digital devices; it is recommended that users put away their devices anywhere from 30 minutes to 2 hours before bedtime. It is also recommended that digital devices be charged far away from the bed or even in another room. Chimes, buzzes, or changes in light within the bedroom can wake a person at night, disrupting the sleep cycle and making it harder to feel rested and healthy.

Digital addiction can have an extreme side effect: There have been numerous cases of people, notably nonstop video gamers, who have played for so long without breaks that they have died from starvation, exhaustion, or heart problems. In Taiwan, for example, an 18-year-old named Chuang rented a private room in an internet café and played *Diablo 3* for 40 hours straight. When he finally stood up, he collapsed. The doctors believe he died because he developed a blood clot after sitting in the same spot for too long. In 2005, a man named Lee Seung Seop also died as a result of his digital addiction. After being fired from his job when his gaming interfered with his work, he entered an internet café and played *StarCraft* for 50 hours. Shortly thereafter, he collapsed and died from exhaustion and dehydration.

Texting and Driving

Texting while driving is another huge problem that has grown with the consistent use of mobile devices. The majority of U.S. states have passed laws against this practice. Someone who is caught doing so can be fined, have their license suspended, pay more in car insurance rates, or even face jail time. According to the Department of Motor Vehicles (DMV), in 2014, 26 percent of all car crashes involved cell phone use. The number of people hurt because of cell phone use has continued to rise. In 2016, pedestrian fatalities rose by 11 percent due to an increase in distracted driving.

Certain apps have been designed to combat this problem by blocking texts and calls from coming in while someone is driving, so there is less temptation for people to check their phones. For example, the LifeSaver app uses the phone's sensors to lock the phone when it is moving at driving speeds. Apple has also designed its newest phones with the feature "Do Not Disturb While Driving," which automatically blocks notifications from coming through while a person is in a moving vehicle. Users can either set it up to turn on automatically or trigger it manually when they get in the car. People who had the feature enabled used their phones 8 percent less in 2017.

Signs of an Addiction

Most researchers note that while many people tend to overindulge in digital usage, only a very small portion of people are actually diagnosably addicted. According to Net Addiction Recovery, 8 to 10 percent of technology users are in need of treatment for the overuse of technology.

Marshall Carpenter is one example of someone with a technology addiction. He described his situation: "I was basically living on Dr Pepper, which is packed with caffeine and sugar. I would get weak from not eating but I would only notice it when I got so shaky I stopped being able to think and play [video games] well."[29] At the age of 25, Carpenter was playing video games for 15 hours a day, had lost a sports scholarship, and dropped out of college. He was addicted, and his father broke down his barricaded door in order to get him help. Carpenter went to reSTART, a residential treatment facility for digital addiction. There, Carpenter was not alone in his circumstances. Other young men at the program had lost their jobs, their finances, and—in some cases—even their homes to digital addiction.

Different people become addicted for different reasons. Sometimes the reason is apparent—for example, if someone does not have many friends and is using technology as an emotional substitute—but sometimes there is no apparent underlying reason. It may be due to chemical imbalances in the brain or other disorders, but it can be difficult to pinpoint these causes. For example, someone who has ADHD may use the internet constantly because they are bored and have trouble focusing on one thing. With the internet, they can look at many different websites in a matter of minutes, which suits their distracted attention span. Because of this, they may be misdiagnosed with a digital addiction when in reality, their ability to focus is the problem.

In the early stages of an addiction, it might be difficult for someone to know they are becoming addicted. It may also be difficult for loved ones and friends to tell when a person is overusing, since nearly everyone in today's society uses digital technologies a lot. Alternatively, a person who develops an addiction to digital technologies may hide their problem from their loved ones. For example, a teenager may bring their phone to bed with them and scroll throughout the night without their parents knowing, or a spouse may sit in the car for half an hour and do the same before coming inside.

How to Spot an Addiction

In many ways, the patterns and behaviors of a digital addiction can manifest similarly to other addictions. A 2005 article in *CyberPsychology and Behavior* listed five diagnostic criteria for the presence of digital addiction, which have become the most widely accepted form of diagnosis. These criteria are:

- The individual thinks a lot about times they were online in the past and constantly looks forward to being online again in the future.
- The individual needs to be online in increased amounts of time to feel the same level of satisfaction.
- The individual has made unsuccessful attempts to control or stop their use.
- The individual is irritable when attempting to control use.
- The individual stays online longer than they originally intended.

The signs of a digital addiction are similar to those of other behavioral or substance addictions. One of the most noticeable is that the person begins to spend all their free time engaging in an activity. At first, someone playing a video game might be happy to play for half an hour or so—or enough time to complete one level. Eventually, however, one level is not enough. In order to get the same emotional high, a user has to do better—beat more in a shorter amount of time or get to a certain point in a game.

The behavior may then start to take over other areas of the person's life. For example, a person who is addicted to the internet may stop going out to see friends and family. They may even tell lies in order to get their fix. Dr. Hilarie Cash, an expert in digital addiction, gave an

A person with a digital addiction may begin to withdraw from the people around them to spend more time on their digital devices.

example of a young man who had previously been addicted to an online game called *Everquest* and had promised his wife that he would stay away from it in the future. Cash wrote that "the addiction trumped his will-power and he returned to *Everquest*, only now he did it in secret. He went to extraordinary lengths to keep his secret, pretending to go to work, making up stories about his work day after he had been fired, paying their bills with credit cards, and so on."[30] Eventually, the couple's growing debt caused the man to feel suicidal, so he confessed to his wife and she helped him get treatment.

A person with an addiction may also stop taking care of themselves: They may stop keeping up on personal hygiene or stop exercising. An addiction may also affect a person's school or work life; a student's grades may drop, or an employee may stop completing satisfactory work. They may also lose interest in other hobbies and activities they previously enjoyed, which can have a negative effect on their social life and emotional state. If they feel unable to stop their online activity despite experiencing all these problems, then their behavior can be deemed an addiction.

Sometimes loved ones may ask a person with a digital addiction to put their device away. Generally, this kind of request is met with avoidance or frustration. Digital addictions harm relationships as the person with the addiction starts to prioritize their time with their devices above other things and people in their lives. Other signs a person may have a digital addiction include, but are not limited to, extreme tiredness, weight gain or loss, and irritability—especially if it is suggested that they have an addiction.

Other Problems

One of the most common reasons why people develop any addiction, including a digital one, is because they are using the behavior or substance to distract themselves from other problems in their life. In fact, there is a strong correlation between digital addiction and depression. There is also evidence that many people with digital addiction have other mental health issues. Researchers at San Francisco State University believe a lack of body language and face-to-face communication, along with less time to mentally relax, contributes to higher levels of loneliness in people. In November 2018, a link between social media use and mental health issues was identified in a study by the University of Pennsylvania. By following two groups of students—those who were able to use social media websites as they normally did and those whose use the researchers restricted—the study found that people who spent more time on social media websites had higher levels of depression at the end of the study.

Researcher Amanda Oldt, who worked on a study involving college students from McMaster University, noted, "If you are trying to treat someone for an addiction when in fact they are anxious or depressed, then you may be going down the wrong route."[31] With mental health issues, it is important to make sure the right problem is being addressed.

ISOLATING OR CONNECTING?

"There's this idea that maybe people would become more social and more in touch with friends and family if they didn't have use of the internet, but I think that's really mistaken ... Most people using the internet are actually more social than those who are not using the internet."

—William Dutton, researcher at Michigan State University and author of *Society and the Internet*

Quoted in Rachel Nuwer, "What if the Internet Stopped Working for a Day?," BBC, February 7, 2017. www.bbc.com/future/story/20170207-what-if-the-internet-stopped-for-a-day.

Seeking Help

It can be hard to evaluate the depth of a digital addiction, and once an addiction takes hold, it can be hard to treat. Because every person's situation is different, it is important for a person with an addiction to have customized care. Different solutions can have varying results for different people. Sometimes a digital detox and strict regimen at home may be enough. In other cases, a person may be so deep into a behavioral addiction that it is extremely hard to break the cycle, even if they are actively trying and seeking help from supportive family and friends. This is not a failing on the individual's part because addiction is a disease, not a choice. In a case such as this, it is extremely important for the individual to get help from a professional. This might include outpatient therapy, where the patient continues life as normal but sees a therapist regularly. It can also involve inpatient therapy, where they check into a rehabilitation center so they can be monitored by the staff. There are many different varieties of therapy, and different approaches work for different people.

Cognitive behavioral therapy (CBT) was originally developed as a way to treat alcoholism and has since been adapted to all kinds of addictions and other mental illnesses. CBT focuses on anticipating problems and using strategies to resist temptations. It helps patients increase their self-control by giving them healthier coping methods than the object of their addiction. The idea is that by identifying and changing negative thought patterns, patients can change the way they feel about certain things. For example, if someone who is frequently lonely finds themselves thinking, "I'm worthless and no one likes me," they can replace that thought with something such as, "I have several good friends and if I join a group I'm interested in, I can make more." With that type of control over their emotions, they tend to be less likely to feel the need to turn to a substance or behavior to soothe themselves. Therapists who use CBT are often problem-focused and goal-oriented.

Motivational interviewing is another therapy style that focuses on helping a person find strength through their internal feelings. Research has shown that this approach helps people who may be unwilling to make changes in their life unless they have a concrete reason to do so. Examples of a motivation might be a person wanting to beat their addiction because they do not want their family to be upset or because they want to return to work or school. This can be a relatively short type of therapy, since once a person identifies their motivation, they can utilize it.

A different type of therapy called contingency management has been proven to work in drug rehab studies. In this type of therapy, people are given rewards for keeping on track, such as vouchers for goods and services or a chance to win money. Patients therefore are rewarded for good behavior with positive reinforcement. However, it is controversial because critics suggest that this type of therapy can be expensive to provide, and skeptics believe that once the reward is

Group therapy is just one option that may give a person struggling with an addiction the support they need to get better.

no longer available, there will be no incentive for the person not to return to their addiction.

Most types of therapy can be done either one-on-one or in a group. Group therapy can be helpful for people because people who struggle with addictions can talk to one another in a safe and peer-supported atmosphere. Other people in the group not only understand what a person with an addiction is going through, they often also provide accountability. This makes it easier for someone not to give up on therapy because they know other people are rooting for them to succeed. Someone may attend only one or two group therapy sessions and work individually with a therapist the rest of the time, or they may attend regularly. Typically, regular group therapy patients attend more frequently in the beginning stages of treatment and then later only as necessary.

Inpatient Treatment

In the most serious cases, a person may need help from trained professionals in a location that is designed specifically for recovering from addiction. In the United States, the options for digital addiction rehabalitiation centers are growing. Many of these programs recognize that sometimes a person has to go "cold turkey," meaning they completely stop using what fuels their addiction. In the case of digital addiction, this means a person must be away from technology for a time. Inpatient facilities are especially helpful in this case because they can be designed specifically to avoid technology, which is unique in today's society and difficult for someone to do on their own. On average, these programs last between 28 and 90 days. They come in many different varieties; for example, reSTART mainly treats young men by having very little technology on the premises and by encouraging them to hike, take care of animals, and engage in social games such as frisbee, volleyball, or board games. According to the *Guardian*, "In many ways, reSTART is like any other rehab place: first detox, and then face underlying mental health problems, personality traits or life traumas that fuel the dependency and learn how to communicate about that, and finally figure out how to abstain or use in moderation."[32] Alternatively, there are short-term programs such as the one at Bradford Regional Medical Center in central Pennsylvania. In this nine-day program, adult patients take classes located inside the addiction wing of the hospital.

A digital addiction rehab center may encourage patients to get outside and connect with the natural world as well as with other people in the program.

Often in programs of this type, a patient will transition from inpatient to outpatient, meaning that after a set amount of time, they go back to living at home but still continue to be involved in the program. This helps prevent the person from relapsing by giving them access to professional help and support.

Living in a Digital World

A person does not need to give up all digital technologies for fear of becoming addicted as long as they make informed choices about how their time is spent during the day. As Marguerite Darlington pointed out in an article for *Rewire*, "You can be a social media star and not be addicted to digital devices: addiction has more to do with how a device or substance affects your day-to-day life."[33]

Some people see the current overuse of technology as a learning curve—something people will work out for themselves after they get used to having it in their everyday lives. Clive Thompson believes that once people have a better idea of how to use the tools they have, human understanding and productivity will be better off. He wrote, "One of the greatest challenges of today's digital thinking tools is knowing when not to use them, and when to rely on the powers of older and slower technologies, like paper and books."[34] He believes that while digital technologies are very useful, they should be used responsibly.

Others think digital technologies should be redesigned with fewer distracting features and more components that work together with the larger world. Some people believe regulations need to be put in place to limit how people sell and use technology.

A Global Problem

Many countries around the world take digital addiction seriously, and many governments consider technology addiction

> ## INFORMATION WITHOUT APPLICATION IS MEANINGLESS
>
> "We're constantly losing the information that's just come in—we're constantly replacing it, and there's no place to hold what you've already gotten. It makes for a very superficial experience; you've only got whatever's in your mind at the moment ... You end up feeling overwhelmed because what you have is an endless amount of facts without a way of connecting them into a meaningful story."
>
> —Tony Schwartz, productivity expert, on the drawbacks of having Google constantly accessible

Quoted in Carolyn Gregoire, "How to Not Be a Slave to Technology," *Huffington Post*, last updated August 23, 2013. www.huffpost.com/entry/why-you-should-do-less-to_n_3635679.

to be a growing health problem. Singapore, for example, has implemented active "cyber wellness" campaigns against digital addiction, which are designed for preschool children. Along with India, South Korea, China, and Taiwan, Singapore has also opened technology addiction centers. In Taiwan, the government created a ban on digital technology of any kind for children under the age of two. A parent who breaks this ban may be fined severely.

As part of his 2017 election campaign, French president Emmanuel Macron promised new laws to ban devices during school hours. In September 2018, those laws began to take effect, giving schools the ability to partially or totally ban cell phone use. In most cases, this means students are not allowed to use their phones, tablets, or other devices at all during school hours, including at lunch. France's education minister Jean-Michel Blanquer called the ban a "law for the 21st century."[35]

Other people are taking the matter into their own hands. In 2016, Maryland mother of two Cindy Eckward launched a grassroots campaign to create legislation to limit screen time in schools. The organization she created is called Screens

Inside a Chinese Technology-Free Boot Camp

In China, the first country in the world to label online addiction as a disorder, many young people with an internet addiction are placed in technology-free boot camps. These camps have received praise from some and criticism from others for their prison-like accommodations. Reports have surfaced that some camps swear at and beat the young adults. The *Washington Post* reported in 2016 that "some were ordered to stand still all night or lie down on their stomachs in snow-covered fields in the winter … In 2009, a 15-year-old boy … died after being beaten by trainers two days after arriving [at] a camp treating Internet addiction."[1]

Fortunately, other camps are not so inhumane. At one camp near Shanghai, young adults are given classes in ballet, music, stand-up comedy, and more. As one of the art teachers at the camp said, "Some parents use only severe methods, like beating or scolding, towards their children. They have no idea how to guide their kids into a beautiful world."[2] However, they are also required to walk 186 miles (300 km) at least three times per year, which some of the teens have complained about. Many are also dropped off at the camp with no warning from their parents. Some of the teens who have attended this camp feel imprisoned, but others are grateful for the chance to detox from their digital addiction.

1. Simon Denyer and Gu Jinglu, "Chinese Teen Starves Mother to Death in Fury at Brutal Internet Addiction Boot Camp," *Washington Post*, September 22, 2016. www.washingtonpost.com/news/worldviews/wp/2016/09/22/chinese-teen-starves-mother-to-death-in-fury-at-brutal-internet-addiction-boot-camp/?utm_term=.7013e9783ac5.
2. Quoted in Tom Phillips, "'Electronic Heroin': China's Boot Camps Get Tough on Internet Addicts," *Guardian*, August 28, 2017. www.theguardian.com/world/2017/aug/28/electronic-heroin-china-boot-camps-internet-addicts.

and Kids, and it asks parents, teachers, and schools to take responsibility for students' health.

Others believe regulations are not a great solution. As Susan Greenfield wrote, "Another argument sometimes used

French president Emmanuel Macron helped bring new laws into effect that ban the use of cell phones in school.

to dismiss any concerns about digital culture is the idea that we'll muddle through as long as appropriate regulation is in place."[36] However, she noted, regulations are often only responses to events. Regulations cannot imagine "the best uses to which new technologies can be put."[37] A better approach, Greenfield argued, is to be proactive from the start by questioning why and how things are used, both in classrooms and in everyday life.

No Escape

One of the hardest things about having a digital addiction is that there is no good way to escape from digital technologies in everyday life. While people with other substance or behavioral addictions can try to avoid places that are tempting or triggering, a person with a digital addiction has to live in a world where they are essentially required to use a phone and computer regularly. The social and financial costs of not having one or both of these devices are increasing all the time. For example, many companies require their employees to know how to use a computer and to be reachable by phone or email. Children and teens are also frequently required to use the internet for research papers and other schoolwork, and parents do not generally have a say in the ways their child's school uses technology. Fortunately, there are steps someone with a digital addiction can take to protect themselves, starting with creating a healthy environment where their needs are more likely to be met offline.

The best solution to digital addiction is prevention. Because it is so easy to become addicted to technology, people must take care to engage with technology in a smart way in order to avoid becoming addicted in the first place. This means setting limits on time spent on digital technologies as well as personalizing their technology to be the least intrusive it can be—for example, by turning off all but the most important notifications.

Getting Offline

For someone suffering from a digital addiction, the idea of going without technological devices is extremely stressful. Nomophobia, a contraction of the phrase "no-mobile-phone phobia," is "the fear of being without a mobile device, or beyond mobile phone contact."[38] Although this is not a phobia that is officially recognized by mental health professionals, many people can relate to the fear of being without a phone. Researchers from the City University of Hong Kong in China and the Sungkyunkwan University in Seoul, South Korea,

Using physical versions of programs people often rely on their phones for, such as a calendar or notebook, can help someone reduce their reliance on digital technology.

came to the conclusion that as people use smartphones and other devices, the devices start to feel almost like an extension of the user, which makes people more attached to them.

Although some people believe nomophobia is a serious problem, other researchers have pointed out that context is important. According to researcher William Dutton, author of the book *Society and the Internet*, socioeconomic status has a lot to do with how attached someone may become to their digital devices. In 1998, a satellite failure caused nearly all of the pagers in the United States to stop working. When

The Dangers of Digital Addiction

Dutton surveyed 250 people in Los Angeles, California, who were affected by this outage, he found that people who had white-collar jobs with comfortable, reliable incomes saw the event as an unexpected vacation day. In contrast, blue-collar workers such as plumbers or carpenters who had less steady incomes and could only be notified of new job opportunities through their pagers found the outage very stressful, as they were losing money and had little savings to fall back on.

Pagers were widely used in the 1990s before cell phones became common. They were used to alert someone that another person wanted to contact them. After receiving the alert, they could use a nearby phone to get more information about why they were being contacted.

Furthermore, single mothers whose children were at daycare were worried that they would not be able to be reached if their children needed them. Dutton concluded that people did not become attached to the device itself as much as the ways that device made life easier for them.

> **NOT GOING AWAY**
>
> "Unless we have a disaster that triggers a major shift in usage, the convenience and benefits of connectivity will continue to attract users. Evidence suggests that people value convenience today over possible future negative outcomes."
>
> –David Clark, MIT senior research scientist
>
> Quoted in Christianna Silva, "The Internet of Things Is Becoming More Difficult to Escape," NPR, June 6, 2017. www.npr.org/sections/alltechconsidered/2017/06/06/531747037/the-internet-of-things-is-becoming-more-difficult-to-escape.

Now that phones allow people to do a variety of different things, they can be harder to put down. Different approaches for getting off the phone—and for not feeling FOMO about it—work for different people. Someone who has a milder addiction might benefit from keeping a journal, engaging in mindfulness practices, or visiting a support group. According to Dr. Ronald Alexander, "One of the first steps in dealing with addiction is to discover the emotional cause of it."[39] If a person can figure out what digital technologies are standing in for, they can choose to fill their time with different activities that fill the same need and are more productive.

Creating Healthy Boundaries

A person with a digital addiction who wants to recover should remove as much temptation as possible from their life. This could include deleting accounts that are not useful. If someone is addicted to their email, for example, they might unsubscribe from all email sources that send junk. This way, their inbox is less likely to be crowded. A person who is addicted to cell phone games might delete most or all of their game apps.

Someone who finds themselves aimlessly surfing the internet for hours might consider using a news aggregator, which is an app that puts relevant web content into one location for easy viewing. This way, a person can check the news from all their favorite websites while resisting the temptation to click through to other links, which could result in a longer internet session than was originally intended. Some popular news aggregator apps include Feedly, News360, AllTop, the Skimm, and Google News.

THE WORLD CAN WAIT

"Once my mind stopped anticipating a new text message or social media interaction every five minutes, it seemed to grow calmer, and I felt more creative. The only disappointing thing was the discovery, when I turned my phone back on each day, that there were few matters in my life so urgent that they couldn't wait two or three hours for a response."

—Katz Marlin, journalist

Katz Marlin, "Setting Boundaries with Your Phone—On Your Own Terms," Headspace, accessed on January 28, 2019. www.headspace.com/blog/2017/06/24/setting-phone-boundaries/.

Another important step a person who has a digital addiction can take is to turn off push notifications for everything that is not important. Notifications are designed to distract a person from whatever they were doing by calling their attention to their phone. According to Rosie Spinks of *Quartzy* magazine, "If you want to improve your mental health, your goal with push notifications should be to get to a point where, when you receive one, it contains time-sensitive information that is relevant to the next hour of your life—and thus worth the interruption."[40] Someone may also schedule a few hours when devices are turned off and put away. Arianna Huffington, founder of the *Huffington Post*, described four practices that help her experience more mindfulness throughout the day: not charging her phone in her bedroom while she is sleeping, taking 10 minutes in the morning before looking at technology to set an intention for the day, taking one device-free vacation each year, and leaving the phone behind on purpose sometimes.

Turning off push notifications is a great first step in reducing digital use.

Often, a person will turn to digital technologies when boredom sets in. Boredom, in general, is seen as a negative feeling: It can trigger negative emotions, and it is natural for people to want to remove themselves from those kinds of feelings. However, boredom can actually be a powerful motivational tool. Some of the best creative moments come from a state of boredom. Indeed, many artists, scientists, and thinkers see boredom as a good thing. Peter Bregman, the CEO of a company that helps other businesses create positive behavioral change in their employees, wrote, "Being bored is a precious thing, a state of mind we should pursue. Once boredom sets in, our minds begin to wander, looking for something exciting, something interesting to land on. And that's where creativity arises."[41] By creating slots of time that are free of digital technology and work, a person has the time to create.

A person with a mild digital addiction may structure an hour of this sort of time in a day. It might be beneficial to

It may be helpful for a person struggling with their digital use to schedule an hour of technology-free time during their day.

keep the phone in another room or download an app that blocks scrolling for a set amount of time. One such app is called Forest. It allows people to block whichever apps they choose for up to two hours at a time. Each time they set the timer, they grow a digital tree; if they use any of the apps they blocked, their tree dies. Another app by the same creators, called SleepTown, starts up at the user's specified bedtime and builds a town throughout the night. If the person uses their phone during this time, their buildings collapse. This gamelike motivation may be enough for someone with a mild addiction, but others may benefit from apps that make it impossible for someone to use certain apps or use their phone at all for set periods of time, such as Offtime or Flipd.

Mindfulness practices are another great tool for pursuing a healthy and balanced lifestyle. Mindfulness is the art of being present in life, and studies have shown that mindfulness activities can actually reshape the brain. According to a Harvard-affiliated research study, structural differences were found after an eight-week mindfulness-based stress reduction program at the University of Massachusetts Center for Mindfulness. The researchers used magnetic resonance imaging (MRI) to look at the participants' brains before and after the program. The MRIs showed increased gray-matter density in the hippocampus, an area of the brain known to be important for learning and memory, and in brain structures associated with self-awareness and compassion. Britta Hölzel, one of the researchers, said, "It is fascinating to see the brain's plasticity and that, by practicing meditation, we can play an active role in changing the brain and can increase our well-being and quality of life."[42]

A person struggling with their digital use can often enlist the help of friends and family—a team of people who are on their side and want them to live a healthy life. For example, it is a lot easier to follow technology rules in a house when everyone abides by them and holds others accountable. One game that is popular with families and friends is to put phones facedown on the table during dinner. The first person to reach for their device either has to do the dishes or pay for the meal if eating out. Other families have a no-technology policy starting an hour before bed.

Sometimes it is helpful for friends or family members to keep one another accountable. If more than one person engages in technology-free time, it is more likely that everyone will follow through.

Changing the Relationship

When the environment is altered and when people have the tools necessary to create a positive lifestyle and positive mental health, the risks of digital addiction decrease. That

What Would Happen if the Internet Shut Down?

When people are dependent on something, going without it can feel strange or unsettling. Many people believe that if the internet shut down, even temporarily, people around the world would not be able to function. However, some experts disagree. In 2008, researcher Scott Borg of the nonprofit United States Cyber Consequences Unit was asked by the U.S. Department of Homeland Security to analyze what might happen to the economy and to society if the internet were to shut down for several days. Borg and his team studied the effects of past outages that lasted four days or fewer and discovered that the damage was far less than people might expect. Most businesses did not suffer, he reported, and most people treated the outage as an unexpected work vacation. People were also still able to travel, but an outage that lasts longer than four days would make it increasingly difficult for plane and train schedules to be coordinated.

Other researchers have suggested that the main effect of an internet outage on the general population is likely to be feelings of isolation and loneliness. As Stine Lomborg of the University of Copenhagen noted, "It's not like we'd be more likely to speak to strangers at the bus stop if we didn't have our smartphones."[1] Instead, people would likely be distressed that they could not reach their family and friends through email and social media.

1. Quoted in Rachel Nuwer, "What if the Internet Stopped Working for a Day?," BBC, February 7, 2017. www.bbc.com/future/story/20170207-what-if-the-internet-stopped-for-a-day.

is a start, but there is still a problem that needs to be solved: the commercialization of technology and the ways companies deliberately try to get people addicted. Clive Thompson wrote, "Realistically, I suspect there's no killer app to end distraction. The downsides of being highly networked are constitutionally tied to the benefits. The only way we can reduce the negative side effects is by changing our relationship to the digital environment, both as a society and as individuals."[43]

Being mindful of digital use is the first step toward creating a healthy conversation about this issue. People who are aware of the digital landscape and its effect on people's lives can create the next wave of devices that are designed and used in ways that help humans rather than harming them.

NOTES

Introduction: Changing Times

1. Clive Thompson, *Smarter Than You Think: How Technology Is Changing Our Minds for the Better*. New York, NY: Penguin Press, 2013, p. 6.

2. John H. Lienhard, "What People Said About Books in 1498," University of Houston, 1998. www.uh.edu/engines/indiana.htm.

3. Susan Greenfield, *Mind Change: How Digital Technologies Are Leaving Their Mark on Our Brains*. New York, NY: Random House, 2015, p. 18.

4. Quoted in Nick Bilton, "Steve Jobs Was a Low-Tech Parent," *New York Times*, September 10, 2014. www.nytimes.com/2014/09/11/fashion/steve-jobs-apple-was-a-low-tech-parent.html?_r=0.

5. Chris Weller, "Silicon Valley Parents Are Raising Their Kids Tech-Free—and It Should Be a Red Flag," *Business Insider*, February 18, 2018. www.businessinsider.com/silicon-valley-parents-raising-their-kids-tech-free-red-flag-2018-2.

Chapter 1: Technology in the Modern Age

6. Quoted in "Surgical Theater and UCSF Benioff Children's Hospital Oakland Chief of Surgery, Kurtis Auguste, MD, to Be Featured on The Doctors CBS Network Show," *L.A. Biz*, September 17, 2018. www.bizjournals.com/los-angeles/prnewswire/press_releases/California/2018/09/17/UN10182.

Chapter 2: What Is an Addiction?

7. Adam Alter, *Irresistible: The Rise of Addictive Technology and the Business of Keeping Us Hooked*. New York, NY: Penguin Press, 2017, p. 29.

8. "Definition of Addiction," American Society of Addiction Medicine, April 12, 2011. www.asam.org/resources/definition-of-addiction.

9. "Addiction as a Disease," Center on Addiction, last updated April 14, 2017. www.centeronaddiction.org/what-addiction/addiction-disease.

10. James Clear, "How Vietnam War Veterans Broke Their Heroin Addictions," from *Atomic Habits: An Easy & Proven Way to Build Good Habits & Break Bad Ones*. New York, NY: Avery, 2018. jamesclear.com/heroin-habits.

11. Alter, *Irresistible*, p. 25.

12. Jon E. Grant, Brian L. Odlaug, and Samuel R. Chamberlain, "What Is a Behavioral Addiction?," *Psychology Today*, June 27, 2016. www.psychologytoday.com/us/blog/why-cant-i-stop/201606/what-is-behavioral-addiction.

13. "Gaming Disorder," World Health Organization, September 2018. www.who.int/features/qa/gaming-disorder/en/.

14. Quoted in Jane Wakefield, "Gaming Addiction Classified as Disorder by WHO," BBC, January 2, 2018. www.bbc.com/news/technology-42541404.

15. Quoted in Isobel Asher Hamilton, "There's Zero Compelling Evidence Showing Tech Is as Addictive as Cocaine, According to Scientists," *Business Insider Australia*, July 10, 2018. www.businessinsider.com.au/theres-no-evidence-that-tech-is-as-addictive-as-cocaine-2018-7.

16. Quoted in Hamilton, "There's Zero Compelling Evidence."

Chapter 3: Technology Taking Over

17. Alter, *Irresistible*, p. 3.

18. Quoted in Cari Romm, "Americans Are More Afraid of Robots Than Death," *The Atlantic*, October 16, 2015. www.theatlantic.com/technology/archive/2015/10/americans-are-more-afraid-of-robots-than-death/410929/.

19. Quoted in Vaughan Bell, "Don't Touch That Dial!," *Slate*, February 15, 2010. slate.com/technology/2010/02/a-history-of-media-technology-scares-from-the-printing-press-to-facebook.html.

20. Dennis Rosen, "Watching TV Leads to Obesity," *Psychology Today*, August 13, 2009. www.psychologytoday.com/us/blog/sleeping-angels/200908/watching-tv-leads-obesity.

21. Joe Clement and Matt Miles, *Screen Schooled: Two Veteran Teachers Expose How Technology Overuse Is Making Our Kids Dumber*. Chicago, IL: Chicago Review Press, 2018, p. 19.

22. Téa Silvestre Godfrey, "#FollowFriday Much? My Love-Hate Relationship with Fan Base-Building Tactics," *Story Bistro*, January 31, 2019. storybistro.com/follow-friday-much-how-twitter-culture-can-help-or-hurt-relationships/.

23. Quoted in Marguerite Darlington, "This Is What Digital Addiction Looks Like," *Rewire*, December 12, 2017. www.rewire.org/living/digital-addiction/.

24. Quoted in Greenfield, *Mind Change*, p. 54.

25. Natasha Singer, "How Google Took Over the Classroom," *New York Times*, May 13, 2017. www.nytimes.com/2017/05/13/technology/google-education-chromebooks-schools.html.

26. Quoted in Alon Shwartz, "Our Kids Are Losing Their Empathy & Technology Has a Lot to Do with It," Medium, September 19, 2017. medium.com/@alonshwartz/our-kids-are-losing-their-empathy-technology-has-a-lot-to-do-with-it-7f18f2654a7f.

27. Jesse Singal, "Crowdfunding for Medical Bills Shows the Limits of Empathy," *The Cut*, March 14, 2017. www.thecut.com/2017/03/crowdfunding-for-medical-bills-shows-the-limits-of-empathy.html.

28. "Smartphone Addiction Creates Imbalance in Brain," Radiological Society of North America, November 30, 2017. press.rsna.org/timssnet/media/pressreleases/14_pr_target.cfm?id=1989.

Chapter 4: Signs of an Addiction

29. Quoted in Joanna Walters, "Inside the Rehab Saving Young Men from Their Internet Addiction," *Guardian*, June 16, 2017. www.theguardian.com/technology/2017/jun/16/internet-addiction-gaming-restart-therapy-washington.

30. Hilarie Cash, "Why Is It so Hard to Believe in a Behavioral Addiction?," *Psychology Today*, November 20, 2011. www.psychologytoday.com/us/blog/digital-addiction/201111/why-is-it-so-hard-believe-in-behavioral-addiction.

31. Quoted in "Internet Addiction Linked to Depression, Anxiety, ADHD in College Students," Healio, September 19, 2016. www.healio.com/psychiatry/pediatrics/news/online/%7B949eed00-3010-430a-842b-05393d046c32%7D/internet-addiction-linked-to-depression-anxiety-adhd-in-college-students.

32. Walters, "Inside the Rehab Saving Young Men."

Chapter 5: Living in a Digital World

33. Darlington, "This Is What Digital Addiction Looks Like."

34. Thompson, *Smarter Than You Think*, p. 14.

35. Quoted in Jakub Lewandowski, "Back to School Without Mobile Phones: France Imposes Nationwide Ban," *Newsweek*, September 4, 2018. www.newsweek.com/back-school-without-mobile-phones-france-imposes-nationwide-ban-1104060.

36. Greenfield, *Mind Change*, p. 9.

37. Greenfield, *Mind Change*, p. 10.

38. Tim Elmore, "Nomophobia: A Rising Trend in Students," *Psychology Today*, September 18, 2014. www.psychologytoday.com/us/blog/artificial-maturity/201409/nomophobia-rising-trend-in-students.

39. Ronald Alexander, "Mindfulness Meditation & Addiction," *Psychology Today*, April 16, 2010. www.psychologytoday.com/us/blog/the-wise-open-mind/201004/mindfulness-meditation-addiction.

40. Rosie Spinks, "One Simple Thing You Can Do for Better Mental Health: Turn Off Your Push Notifications," *Quartzy*, October 6, 2018. qz.com/quartzy/1416069/turn-off-push-notifications-for-better-mental-health/.

41. Peter Bregman, "Why I Returned My iPad," *Harvard Business Review*, June 16, 2010. hbr.org/2010/06/why-i-returned-my-ipad.html.

42. Quoted in Sue McGreevy, "Eight Weeks to a Better Brain: Meditation Study Shows Changes Associated with Awareness, Stress," *Harvard Gazette*, March 8, 2016. news.harvard.edu/gazette/story/2011/01/eight-weeks-to-a-better-brain/.

43. Thompson, *Smarter Than You Think*, p. 137.

DISCUSSION QUESTIONS

Chapter 1: Technology in the Modern Age

1. How has technology changed in your lifetime?
2. What are some positive and negative effects technology has had on you?
3. How often do you use digital technologies?

Chapter 2: What Is an Addiction?

1. Do you believe digital addiction is a real addiction? Why or why not?
2. How would the world today be different without digital technologies?
3. Do you feel like you or anyone you know is addicted to digital technologies? Why or why not?

Chapter 3: Technology Taking Over

1. Discuss what you think about the design of digital technologies you use and how that might play a part in them becoming addictive.
2. Do you think smartphones are more problematic than televisions?
3. What do you think of using Google products in the classroom?

Chapter 4: Signs of an Addiction

1. When does digital overuse turn into an addiction?
2. Why do you think society has a negative view of people with addictions?
3. What do you believe might be the most effective way to treat someone who is struggling with a digital addiction?

Chapter 5: Living in a Digital World

1. How can you put limits on digital technology use in your life?
2. Do you think government regulations on technology use can be helpful?
3. How much of a problem do you think digital overuse and addiction are in today's society?

ORGANIZATIONS TO CONTACT

FCD Prevention Works
29 Crafts Street, Suite 150
Newton, MA 02458
(617) 964-9300
schools@fcd.org
fcd.org
> Affiliated with the Hazelden Betty Ford Foundation, FCD is a nonprofit, school-based substance abuse prevention organization. Its website offers a lot of information on addiction in general.

Illinois Institute for Addiction Recovery
5409 N. Knoxville Avenue
Peoria, IL 61614
(800) 522-3784
PIA_ARCReferral@unitypoint.org
www.addictionrecov.org
> The institute specializes in addiction recovery, and it is especially knowledgeable in internet and video game addiction.

Reboot & Recover
2801 S. Federal Highway #350043
Fort Lauderdale, FL 33316
(786) 505-6419
information@rebootandrecover.org
www.rebootandrecover.org
> This nonprofit organization provides information and support to teens and adults. Its mission is to encourage people to decrease their screen time. People who are concerned that they may have an addiction can take self-assessments on the website or call the organization to talk about addiction counseling. Always ask a parent or guardian before contacting a treatment facility.

reSTART
1001 290th Avenue SE
Fall City, WA 98024
(800) 682-6934
connect@restartlife.com
netaddictionrecovery.com
> A residential center with the goal of treating digital addiction in adolescents and adults, reSTART offers a lot of information on digital addiction. Its website includes detailed information about the programs that are offered.

FOR MORE INFORMATION

Books

Faust, Daniel R. *The Positive and Negative Impacts of Computers in Society*. New York, NY: PowerKids Press, 2019.
   This book examines the ways technology has changed society, both for the better and for the worse.

Graham, PJ. *Video Game Addiction*. San Diego, CA: ReferencePoint Press, 2019.
   The World Health Organization has designated gaming addiction an official illness. Learn more about how this can affect people.

Kamenetz, Anya. *The Art of Screen Time: How Your Family Can Balance Digital Media & Real Life*. New York, NY: PublicAffairs, 2018.
   Kamenetz presents ways individuals and families can use technology in a responsible, balanced way.

Netzley, Patricia D. *Online Addiction*. San Diego, CA: ReferencePoint Press, 2017.
   Netzley discusses the symptoms and treatment of an addiction to the internet.

Thompson, Clive. *Smarter Than You Think: How Technology Is Changing Our Minds for the Better*. New York, NY: Penguin Press, 2013.
   Thompson believes digital technologies have the ability to make humans smarter—if used in the right way.

Websites

Best Life: "20 Signs You're Addicted to Your Smartphone"
bestlifeonline.com/smartphone-addiction
    This article offers information to let people know if they should consider cutting back on their screen time.

Center for Internet and Technology Addiction: Digital Distraction Test
virtual-addiction.com/digital-distraction-test
    Put together by The Center for Internet and Technology Addiction, this test allows people to rate their own digital technology use—a useful tool in self-evaluation.

Sleep.org
sleep.org
    This website is dedicated to sleep health. As digital addiction is especially known to impact a person's sleep patterns, it is helpful to know why a good night's rest is so important.

TechAddiction
www.techaddiction.ca
    For people who may have an addiction to their computer, the internet, or video games, this website is a good source of information.

Time to Log Off
www.itstimetologoff.com
    This website discusses the different types of digital addiction and presents strategies for a digital detox.

INDEX

A

Advanced Research Projects Agency Network (ARPANET), 16
Alexander, Ronald, 81
Alter, Adam, 26, 42, 45
American Telegraph and Telephone Company (AT&T), 18
Apple, 8, 15, 42, 63
apps, 13, 25, 41–42, 45, 50, 61–62, 81–82, 85
artificial intelligence (AI), 13, 52–53
Auguste, Kurtis, 13

B

Bader, Christopher, 43
behavioral addictions, 32–33, 35–36, 69, 78
Bell, Alexander Graham, 18, 20
Bell, Gordon, 50, 52
Blanquer, Jean-Michel, 75
blue light, 60
Borba, Michele, 56
boredom, 30, 83–84
brains, 13, 22–24, 26–27, 32–35, 37–38, 45, 49–50, 52, 56, 59, 64, 85
Bregman, Peter, 84

C

Carpenter, Marshall, 64
Cash, Hilarie, 66–67
cell phones, 21–23, 25, 33, 62, 75, 77
cell towers, 17, 21
Clark, David, 81
Clear, James, 30
Clement, Joe, 43, 54
cognitive behavioral therapy (CBT), 59, 69
concentration, 57
contingency management, 70
Cruger, Matthew, 32

D

Darlington, Marguerite, 74
dependency, 22, 25–26, 35, 48, 72
depression, 36, 38, 60, 67–68
diagnoses, 35–36, 64–65
Diagnostic and Statistical Manual of Mental Disorders (DSM), 35–36
Digital Subscriber Line (DSL), 16
Dolan, Paul, 46
dopamine, 27, 33–35, 38, 45
driving, 62–63
Dutton, William, 68, 79–81

Index

E
Eckward, Cindy, 75
education, 12, 15, 36, 52, 54–55, 75
empathy, 56–58

F
fears, 6–8, 23, 38, 43, 46, 56, 74, 78
fiber optics, 11, 19

G
genes, 26–27, 49
Gessner, Conrad, 43
Godfrey, Téa Silvestre, 47
Google, 6, 16, 19, 51, 54–55, 75
Graham, Richard, 36
Greenfield, Susan, 8, 49, 76–77
Griffiths, Mark, 32
group therapy, 70–71

H
Hirsh-Pasek, Kathy, 37
Hölzel, Britta, 85
Huffington, Arianna, 60, 82

I
Information Age, 13–15
intelligent process automation, 13
internet, 10–11, 13, 15–19, 27, 65–66, 78, 82, 87

J
Jobs, Steve, 8

K
Kolb, Bryan, 49
Konrath, Sara, 59

L
learning, 37, 49, 52, 56, 74, 85
Licklider, J. C. R., 16
Lienhard, John H., 7
Lomborg, Stine, 87
loneliness, 68–69, 87

M
Macron, Emmanuel, 75, 77
magnetic resonance imaging (MRI), 85
Marlin, Katz, 82
Martin, Julia, 24
melatonin, 60–61
memory, 7, 22–24, 26, 49–50, 60, 85
mesolimbic dopamine pathway, 33
Meucci, Antonio, 18
microchips, 25
Miles, Matt, 43, 54
mindfulness, 81–82, 85, 88
motivational interviewing, 69

N
Netflix, 47
neuroplasticity, 49
neurotransmitters, 27, 34, 38, 57–59
news aggregators, 82
nomophobia, 78–79
notifications, 45–48, 63, 78, 82–83

O
Oldt, Amanda, 68
Orben, Amy, 38

P
pagers, 79–80
parenting, 37
Pew Research Center, 13, 22, 50
Przybylski, Andrew, 38

R
regulations, 74, 76–77
rehabilitation centers, 30, 69, 71–72
reSTART, 64, 71
Rosen, Dennis, 43

S
satellites, 6, 11, 17, 79
Schmidt, Eric, 18
Schwartz, Tony, 75
Screens and Kids, 75–76
Silicon Valley, 9
sleep, 28, 60–62, 82
social behavior, 40
social media, 12–13, 16, 29, 38, 41, 45–48, 56, 59, 68, 87
socioeconomic status, 79
Socrates, 7
Spinks, Rosie, 82
studies, 9–10, 32–33, 43, 46, 49–50, 56–58, 68, 85
substance addiction, 32, 36, 65

T
technology-free boot camps, 76
teenagers, 57, 59, 65
television, 43–44, 47
Telstar, 6
texting, 38, 62
Thompson, Clive, 7, 50, 52, 74, 87
Transmission Control Protocol/Internet Protocol (TCP/IP), 16
triggers, 26, 38, 78, 83

U
U.S. Postal Service (USPS), 18

V
video games, 33, 41, 49, 58, 62, 64, 66
Vietnam War, 29
violence, 58
virtual reality, 13–14
vocational training, 12

W
Weller, Chris, 9
Wong, Jessica, 33, 48
World Health Organization (WHO), 36
World Wide Web, 16–17

Y
Young, Kimberley, 35
YouTube, 16, 47

PICTURE CREDITS

Cover, p. 61 Syda Productions/Shutterstock.com; p. 9 Uladzik Kryhin/Shutterstock.com; p. 14 Gorodenkoff/Shutterstock.com; p. 17 drserg/Shutterstock.com; p. 19 (top) cigdem/Shutterstock.com; p. 19 (bottom) asharkyu/Shutterstock.com; p. 20 Everett Historical/Shutterstock.com; p. 21 thitiwat chirayutwibul/Shutterstock.com; p. 23 antoniodiaz/Shutterstock.com; p. 28 Zita/Shutterstock.com; p. 29 Stocktrek Images/Stocktrek Images/Getty Images; p. 31 Hero Images/Hero Images/Getty Images; p. 34 logika600/Shutterstock.com; p. 41 REDPIXEL.PL/Shutterstock.com; p. 42 WAYHOME studio/Shutterstock.com; p. 44 Lambert/Getty Images; p. 48 sondem/Shutterstock.com; p. 51 lev radin/Shutterstock.com; p. 53 Monkey Business Images/Shutterstock.com; p. 55 achinthamb/Shutterstock.com; p. 57 Steve Heap/Shutterstock.com; p. 66 Tero Vesalainen/Shutterstock.com; p. 70 wavebreakmedia/Shutterstock.com; p. 72 David Ryder for The Washington Post via Getty Images; p. 77 Drop of Light/Shutterstock.com; p. 79 Dmytro Zinkevych/Shutterstock.com; p. 80 v74/Shutterstock.com; p. 83 Georgejmclittle/Shutterstock.com; p. 84 Andrey_Popov/Shutterstock.com; p. 86 Jacob Lund/Shutterstock.com.

ABOUT THE AUTHOR

Amanda Vink is an author from Buffalo, NY. She has written multiple books for children and young adults. When she is not writing or acting, she enjoys hiking, visiting national parks, and chasing her cat around with a toy. She tends to leave her phone on silent and therefore cannot be trusted to answer incoming calls.